WOVEN

~BOOK 6~

BLENDED

WOVEN

Copyright ©2017 Erica Chilson

Wicked Reads
PO Box 29
Nelson, PA 16940

www.ericachilson.com/wicked-reads

Printed in the United States of America

First Printing, 2018

ISBN-13: 978-0-9979899-7-7
ISBN-10: 0-9979899-7-1

Woven is a story about friendship. **A bromance**.

Rory Essex never made friends his own age. When he moved across the street from Bethany Oman, he was the older kid playing with the baby. Rory befriended Beth's besties– Devon and Essie. But as they got older, puberty struck, and the age-gap got wider. Rory found new friends, older friends. Inappropriate friends who impacted his entire life– Isis, Auggie, and Robin.

Little Bethany Oman finally grew up, and the age-gap shrunk down to nothing. Now she's Bethany Essex, and she wants her husband to reconnect with her soon-to-be married besties. Bethany and Essie are as thick as thieves, so they set their husbands up on a blind-bromance-date.

Rory doesn't realize he's dating Devon– he just finds the guy intoxicating. Hours out of rehab, struggling with bipolar disorder, and a smothering family, Devon wants two things out of life: to feel safe and to feel alive by having fun.

But Devon's version of fun has to be at an extreme. Cops and fast cars, action movies, and manipulative friends are the makings of a livewire, lust-fueled bromance to last the next seventy years...

A NOTE FROM THE WICKED WRITER:

Woven takes place during the weeks following Devon's return from Arizona, showing events from another perspective. During Warped, I felt showing the bromance between Rory and Devon to be in poor taste, feeling it would take away from the bond between Devon and Essie.

Essie and Devon's bond is strong, forged through two decades of friendship and a decade of anguish. Their perspectives were tainted with fear, which is why I decided to write Woven.

Woven is an uplifting story, showing different types of friendship and love, which is why Devon's voice was more positive in the sections of Warped a year later and in the present time (epilogue).

We all need one person to call our own, who we can be stupid around– make mistakes, make a fool of ourselves. A partner in crime. There's no stress in this friendship, because there's no real fear in disappointing them. No fear in losing their trust, their love, or their respect.

Devon needed someone like that, someone Essie couldn't be for him, because the relationship between a husband and wife isn't always easy.

Devon needed a friend, someone who was neither a relative nor one of his victims. Someone he knew inside and out and trusted. Someone who was also connected to Essie.

As a writer, it's difficult to make life choices for characters, knowing it will impact an entire series, maybe even confuse readers, or make them not believe the bonds I've built in earlier books.

I chose Rory because he was a strong character, one who was caring, kind, giving, and filled with hope. He's a guy's guy, but he also compromises. Devon's a difficult person to love, but he also has an intoxicating personality. I felt Rory and Devon would be the perfect counterbalance– the light and the dark.

NAME	Rory Essex	DATE	Planning his wedding reception
PHONE	He never leaves Rush- just knock on the door	EMAIL	Isis does all that shit.
ADDRESS	Rush. Fairport, Massachusetts		
COMMENTS	Rush's burly yet cuddly manager.		
	BFF to the Wayward ones		

NAME	Officer Devon Mason	DATE	Fresh outta rehab
PHONE	Don't call- his phone is monitored and blocked	EMAIL	Not allowed online
ADDRESS	Shithole. Fairport, Massachusetts		
COMMENTS	Suffocating on family		
	Don't allow near pointy objects or stimulants		

NAME	Bethany Oman Essex	DATE	Summer session- psychology major
PHONE	No need to call- Beth will sense you need her	EMAIL	laptop is permanently attached to hands
ADDRESS	Rush. Fairport, Massachusetts		
COMMENTS	Ex-puppy		
	Newly wedded wife. Still wild		

NAME	Essie Prynne	DATE	2nd trimester bun in the oven
PHONE	Cell shut off due to failure to make payment	EMAIL	primpmaster@primp.com
ADDRESS	Shithole. Fairport, Massachusetts		
COMMENTS	Don't stare at her tits		
	Make sure you tip after your free haircut		

NAME	Malcolm Mason	DATE	Currently terrified, always clingy
PHONE	9 1 1	EMAIL	What's that?
ADDRESS	Pink Taco Hut/Batcave Fairport, Massachusetts		
COMMENTS	Don't forget to give him a hug/ask advice		
	Thank him for all Clover's tasty treats		

NAME	Robin Prynne	DATE	Always Plotting
PHONE	Permanently attached to his hand	EMAIL	He uses everyone else's
ADDRESS	Spook House. Fairport, Massachusetts		
COMMENTS	His ears have ears		
	Magician- impregnated his gf with their bf's jizz		

NAME	Isis Mason	DATE	1st trimester. Scared
PHONE	Call Rob- he knows where to find Isis	EMAIL	manager@rush.com
ADDRESS	Rush. Fairport, Massachusetts		
COMMENTS	Immaculate conception		
	She bites & scratches		

NAME	Augustus Kline	DATE	Awed & furious
PHONE	1(800)xxxxmod	EMAIL	Ask Willow
ADDRESS	Spook House- currently at Rush		
COMMENTS	Suffering from an existential crisis		
	Guilty- always guilty and ashamed		

NAME	Willow Prynne & Kieren Mason	DATE	Just hanging
PHONE	Revamped &/or Wreck & Ruin	EMAIL	See phone
ADDRESS	Shithole. Fairport, Massachusetts		
COMMENTS	Thank for changing oil for free		
	Bring comics & gaming advice		

NAME	Dexter Hayes	DATE	Tobias Kline
PHONE	Don't call	EMAIL	d_hayes@irs.gov
ADDRESS	#2 Crestview Drive. Dominion, New York		
COMMENTS	Toby's master		
	Intervention mediator		

WOVEN mirrors scenes contained within **WARPED**, set approximately four years prior to present (Warped epilogue) and all of Erica Chilson's series. Three characters from the M&M of Restraint series are shown, taking place in the era of time during Dexter.

WOVEN

❧BOOK 6❧

BLENDED

CHAPTER ONE

Rory Essex

"Do you think we should be adding cheese to the pasta salad?" Eyes cutting to the side, I can't help but chuckle at Beth going over to the dark side of passive-aggressiveness.

"Is that your way of telling me not to put cheese in the salad?" Smirking, I continue to cut up tiny cubes of Cabot Seriously Sharp Cheddar. As punishment for acting like a douche, I toss a big handful in with the pasta and vegetables. If she didn't want the cheese in the salad, she should say so, not play mind games.

Beth's face squishes up with annoyance, but she keeps her trap shut. My wife knows she's getting on my last nerve over this Devon Mason bullshit. The guy just got out of rehab– he's not an invalid. He can eat around my cheese.

"Well, it's just..." Beth trails off as she takes in my peeved expression.

"I'm not adding the summer sausage, am I?" I add to the passive-aggressive mood that has descended on our relationship. "I'm going to put it on a paper plate for us carnivores to enjoy."

So what if a guy loses his shit on his best friends, bawls his eyes out while sobbing the word bisexual, and punches someone in the nuts... I mean, I think Beth is slightly overreacting. But what's a guy to do when he marries a psychology major?

For the past three days, I've been in grin and bear it mode because Beth's walking on eggshells around me, waiting for me to go off like a nuclear warhead.

It's really not a big deal– the more I refuse to talk about it, the odder my wife behaves. Beth being passive-aggressive, that's new.

"It's just…" Beth stares down into the big bowl filled with pasta, dressing, and every vegetable I could find at the farmer's market. "Devon has a sensitive stomach now, and this is our first dinner party. *Ever.*"

Finding her too cute, I shove a piece of cheese into Beth's mouth to shut her up. "I bought out an entire stall at the market to fill Dev's belly." For good measure, I add another handful of cheese to the bowl, and I have ginormous hands. "It's Dev and Essie, not the Queen of England and Pope Francis."

"It makes this real, ya know?" Beth's cheeks heat, pinking beautifully, and my heart warms from the sight. "My best friends are coming to dinner– our first guests in our home since we got married. It's a big deal for me, Rory."

"I know." Leaning over the rolling butcher block, I steal a kiss. If Beth's behavior was only about having guests, I would think her adorable, but my epic meltdown is tainting everything she says and does. "I love you."

Blushing brighter, eyes glowing, Beth pulls away to fiddle with a quart of strawberries. "Are these too sweet, do you think?"

Jesus Christ, enough passive-aggression.

Finding the patience of a saint, I pray Bethany gets over my freak-out and starts treating me as usual. "Everything is organic and all-natural. If Dev can't eat it, he can starve."

"I don't know why you're so mean to him." Beth begins hulling strawberries, all the while I stare at her, totally gobsmacked. She did not just ask me that, did she?

"Where's my wife?" I tease, pretending to look for her around the loft. "Hello, calling Bethany Essex! Where is Bethany Essex? And who is this odd creature standing in our kitchen?"

"Ha-ha, very funny." If Beth's cheeks get any brighter, we're going to have to fetch a fever-reducer. "I know he fucked up, but I love Devon, and I want you to love my friends too. You used to be friends with us when we were little."

"I'm behaving." I gesture around the kitchen with my knife blade, pointing at the hours of chopping I've done, the marinating chicken, and how I did half of the items on my honey-do list, which is attached to the fridge with my Michelangelo's David magnets– David is currently wearing an Indian headdress and leather jacket, with his junk hanging out. I may have spent some time playing dress-up today while Bethany studied. "I look forward to seeing Essie."

"But not Devon," Beth stresses, tossing berries into a bowl with some sugar. Too sweet, remember, so why add more sugar?

I ignore my wife by changing the subject on this highly uncomfortable conversation. She wants me to admit something I've never admitted to myself, which truly makes the woman a mind-reader.

"Should we cover David's junk?" I point with the knife in the general direction of the fridge. "Venus is looking positively overdressed."

"What would Freud say..." Bethany trails off, giggling to herself, and it's my turn to flush bright red. Dammit!

Closing my eyes, I breathe deeply to center myself, then begin snapping string beans with a vengeance.

I don't know what the big deal is– I really don't.

Staring up at the ceiling, with Bethany snoring softly against my chest, I feel content and blissed out, to the point I don't even care that I'm harder than hell. Beth snuggles closer, and I purr in response. My mind drifts off, debating whether or not I want to buy my baby new floor mats or get her professionally detailed. She's glowing beautifully with the new wax job I gave her this afternoon.

Essie and I have been conspiring for the past few days, organizing a wedding reception for Bethany, and Devon just got home from rehab tonight, so I know my peace-filled existence has come to an end.

Pizza, I think I'll have that leftover slice of pizza hiding in the fridge for breakfast, after I wake my wife up with my face between her thighs...

Front door slamming against the wall, my arm automatically clenches Bethany to my chest protectively. After a heartbeat or two, where adrenaline flows through my veins in an intoxicating mix of fear and anticipation, my eyes register Isis stalking toward me in the dark.

One of the downsides of living in a loft is everything is in one big room, with nowhere to hide. "We're naked," I remind my oldest friend. "And sleeping."

There's zero sexual tension between me and the hottest female ever to have walked the earth. Probably has something to do with Isis seeing me through my awkward teenage years. Or maybe how she's watched on with amusement while I've been in every compromising position known to man.

"I've seen the show." Isis gestures to Bethany, and I wince, hating my wife's puppy period at the Playroom. I don't mind that Beth is sexually experienced. It's that she didn't enjoy playacting a puppy that stings. Isis has also seen Bethany in every compromising position too.

There's no shame between Isis and me. None.

"I need you to talk some sense into these fools."

Isis's words register, just as, "These?" rolls off my numb tongue. Behind her, casting a guilty shadow, these fools fill my open doorway. "Just because you're my landlords, it doesn't mean you can show up in the middle of the night and enter my space."

"Pfft... you don't pay rent." Isis scoffs, sitting on the edge of my bed. "Or utilities. Or cable. Or internet. Or garbage. Or... you catch my drift."

"That still doesn't—"

"I'm sorry." Auggie steps forward, looking like a guilty shit. He's treated me oddly since... since— I pretend that didn't happen. He's acted guilty, ashamed, and like he's waiting for me to go postal on his ass.

Unlike Bethany, who tries to be tactful and coaxing to get me to acknowledge what happened, and Auggie, who acts like he kicked my puppy, Rob stabs me with the truth.

"I miss fucking your wife." Rob comes to stand next to my side of the bed, gazing down at Beth with unveiled lust. Tugging up the sheet, I quickly cover Beth's tits. "And Auggie misses fucking you."

"Oh, Jesus Christ!" Isis shouts for me. "Knock it the fuck off— look what you've done. You woke Bethany."

"What's going on?" Drowsy, Beth wiggles in my arms, sheet no longer covering her as she rubs her eyes with a pair of clenched fists. Completely shameless after the Playroom, Beth has no qualms about being naked in front of our friends. "What are you guys doing in here? What time is it?"

"Pretty sure you woke Bethany," Rob stresses to Isis. *"Gorgeous, we've invaded your bedtime because Isis is losing her shit, and she's positive Rory can mediate."*

"Mediate what?" I demand, wishing I could go back to ten minutes ago and flick the deadbolt on the door. *"Exactly when will you wayward fuckers grow up?"*

I was a little fella in a big boy's body when I met the deviant trio on the football field. I was always in the middle of two age-groups of friends, never connecting with anyone my own age. Bethany, Devon, and Essie were too young to hang around once I hit puberty— they were still playing with toys, and Devon started to creep me out. Yet Robin, Auggie, and Isis were too advanced for me. Obviously I made the wrong choice, seeing as how 'these fools' are my best friends.

Clearly bewildered, Auggie's big ass lands in a chair, hand reaching to flick on a lamp. "I don't understand how this happened."

"What?" Beth and I mutter in unison, while sharing a look of utter confusion. If anyone knows Auggie, it's Beth. She's made him the subject of her thesis, for shit's sake.

"I'm pregnant," Isis croaks in a hoarse voice filled with unshed tears.

"What?!" Bethany squawks. *"You're celibate."*

"What did you do?" I demand, glaring at Rob.

"Glad to see you know me so well." Rob pats my shoulder, all the while his eyes never leave Beth's hard nipples. *"Tsk-tsk, gorgeous. I thought you knew us better than that."*

"I don't understand," Auggie moans again, sounding tormented... by Robin. *"How did this happen?"*

"Make Rob explain himself," Isis demands of me, as if anyone can make Robin Prynne fucking mind. Stress is making her delusional. *"Force him to tell the truth."*

"Oh, my fucking Lord." Laughing in disgust, I flop back to the mattress, hands over my eyes. If I don't see them, they're not really here. *"Don't bring your shit to my doorstep."*

Crawling out of the covers, Bethany flashes both Rob and me her ass, and the pink beyond. "Are you okay?" Concerned, she scooches over to Isis's side, wrapping an arm around her.

Just goes to show how off Isis is feeling, because she allows herself to be comforted.

Trying to swallow it down, trying to play pretend, but it's impossible as I lie in my bed listening to my wife comfort my terrified best friend. I was the one who held Isis while she recovered in the hospital after losing their baby. I was the one who comforted both Auggie and Rob as Isis froze them out. I was the one who dealt with the fallout as they fucked a swath through Fairport. I was the one who ignored how much the Playroom hurt Isis on a cellular level. I was the one who knows all of Isis's deepest, darkest fears, fears Robin has now exploited.

Snap.

I motherfucking snap.

Lunging from my cocoon, words spew without any conscious thought on my part. "Everything in the world is not about you guys!" *Fists raised in the air, the louder I yell, the easier it is to drown out Auggie's whining, Isis's crying, and Rob's gloating.*

"Always make it about you. Remember my first football game? You guys decided it would be more fun to kidnap me, saving me from the 'jock life'. I was kicked off the team because Coach didn't believe me, and I really wanted to play. Remember my goddamn graduation? You had a problem at Rush and pulled me out of a party– Jesus, Cathy Rathbone was going to let me screw her that night, after months of seducing her. Remember college? Yeah, of course not, because I didn't go. I've lived life as your shadows, taking on your problems as if they're my own... Let me live my life!"

"Rory." *Bethany reaches out to me, as if I'm the one who's nuts. The terror reflected in her eyes momentarily stuns me.* "You're going to be okay, babe."

Naked, crouching on the floor, bellowing at the people I love the most, I realize I'm crying. "You. Fucked. Me." *Voice breaking on a sob, I release the pain that's been building.* "You fucking knew why that wasn't a good idea, you bastard."

"Rory." *Now Auggie gets in on the soothe Rory off the ledge action. The man is smart enough not to touch me, but he leans forward in the chair to get closer.* "Why wasn't that a good idea?"

"Fuck you, asshole!" I hurl back at Auggie for playing innocent. He knows goddamn well why I abandoned my friends and joined these fools instead. Just like I've never felt a tinge of attraction for Isis, I didn't for Rob or Auggie either. It was a comfort to be around people like me, and be able to play pretend because I didn't want any of them.

I was a late bloomer, but Essie, Devon, and Beth weren't. Our age-gap shrunk, until we were in a cyclone of rampaging hormones, and it confused the piss out of me. Loving Beth was comforting. Finding Essie hot felt natural. Devon's horny swagger creeped me out on a cellular level, so I left to play pretend with people I didn't want.

Glaring, I seethe, "You know why."

Beth's, "Why?" draws me up short, because she doesn't know why— she is innocent. She didn't manipulate me. She didn't use my nature against me. She didn't use our situation to her advantage. She didn't make me face the truth.

"I hate you," I snarl at Auggie, gasping for air as a sob lodges deep in my throat. "We're not talking about this right now. Our best friend is pregnant, and we have to solve it."

"What's going on?" Isis joins the fun, and I know I'm royally fucked now. I can't not answer if she asks.

"Hey." Rob's fingers wrap around my neck, warm palm resting on my nape. "We don't have to go there. This is between you and Beth." See, Rob knows too.

"It's my fault." Auggie turns back into the martyr who arrived earlier. "I was too curious, and I fucked up."

"What's going on?" Beth steps off the bed, naked as the day she was born. "Does this have anything to do with what happened between you and Auggie? You never want to talk about that."

We both ignore Rob's snort.

"I still don't, and I'm not going to right now either." Drawing up to my full height, I try to be commanding. "Everyone who doesn't live in this loft, leave!"

"Rory—" Auggie tries to reason with me.

"No! Damn you. I love Bethany. I always have, and I always will. I'm happy, don't you see that? Blissfully fucking happy. I have the girl of my dreams, and we're building a life together.

You keep trying to get me to acknowledge that you screwed me, and that's not fucking cool, buddy."

"Why?" Isis asks in a soft voice, sounding relieved to problem-solve something that doesn't involve herself. If I was to mediate with Rob and Auggie, then Isis will mediate between me and everyone else. It's how it always goes. "What's going on? Answer me."

"It doesn't matter," I plead, voice breaking, tears spilling down my cheeks. Bethany looks terrified for me for some reason. "I'm happy– this is what I want, and nothing will change it."

"Then why are you crying?" Isis points out because Beth has been rendered speechless.

"Because it's not fair what Auggie did to me–"

"Did to you, or for you?" Robin stresses.

"Don't," I warn, on the verge of snapping. "Don't do this to me."

"I didn't do anything to you that you didn't want," Auggie mutters, knowing damn well that's the motherfucking malfunction. "Just admit it, so we can move on with our lives, and you'll stop acting like a weirdo around me. You blame me, but you were born this way. I didn't change you– I made you acknowledge it."

"Acknowledge what?" Bethany and Isis say in unison, both sounding betrayed. The betrayal of a best friend and husband for keeping secrets.

"It's private," I mutter cowardly, knowing it makes the betrayal sting worse. "I didn't tell them shit." I point at Rob and Auggie. "They just know."

"Know what?" Bethany asks, but I can tell she already figured it out and wants me to say it. Wants me to say it, not because she needs to hear it, but because I need to say it out loud for myself.

"I can't– it's not important." But then I realize who my wife is, how much she loves me, and what she's training to become. Something vital in me relaxes, because the truth will set me free. But the terror of the truth has me crumbling to my knees, sobs wracking my body.

"Don't make me say it. Once it's out, it can't be put back," I warn myself and no one else.

What pain will this cause my wife? What insecurities will form? Will she think I don't want her? Will she worry about what I'm thinking when I'm people-watching?

If I admit it, does that mean the attraction will return? As long as I avoided a few key people, I could play pretend. What happens if I want someone else? It's not that big of a deal when I see a hot girl, because I want my wife like no other. But this isn't something Bethany can give me, and I don't know how to live with the guilt of that. The guilt of wanting someone other than her– the guilt of wanting to explore something I never acknowledged.

It wasn't a problem until Auggie unleashed it in me... hours before Bethany and I got married.

But then I realize it's not about Bethany, and not saying it out loud won't change the fact.

"I'm– I'm bi... I'm bisexual."

CHAPTER TWO

"You're being quiet." Bethany draws me from the memory, and I'm relieved she does. I was about to relive punching Auggie in the nuts, and I couldn't survive it. Last time, I ended up puking afterward.

"Do you think Devon gets sick of chicken?" Ignoring the fact that my wife knows exactly where my head is at, I flinch as Devon's name passes my lips. Bethany misunderstands, but I let her continue to believe what she does because the truth is sickening.

"Devon's trying really hard, Rory," she admonishes me for hating on her friend, when I'm anything but. "What are you getting at about the chicken?"

"I'm not making fun of the guy," I brush it off while placing marinated chicken breasts on the broiler rack. "I mean, his diet is pretty much the same shit, different day. I was really wondering if he ever gets sick of chicken."

Giggling softly, Beth's devious amusement warms my heart. "Ask Dev what happened when he ate his birthday cake." The knock on the door has her eyes going wide and her smile brightening.

As uncomfortable as this makes me feel, I would never deny Bethany anything. I'm not going to be a prick by being rude and unwelcoming. I'll try my best and behave, even if it kills me.

I've been a dick to Devon to keep him off my dick's mind– I can at least admit that to myself. It was a relief when Devon turned into a druggie, because it dimmed that intoxicating magnetism of his. But I've always felt like shit for feeling relieved, like I contributed to his addiction instead of getting my ex-friend help.

I feel so selfish and sick inside when I look at Devon, for a billion reasons over.

"Hey!" Beth calls warmly, opening the front door. Arms are pulling her into a hug before the door is fully open, glittery fingernails fluffing up her hair. "I know, I'm due for a trim."

"We'll get you fixed up tomorrow." Essie pulls away from my wife, then flashes me a smile and waves in my direction. "Maybe we'll add a few honey highlights this time."

Catching myself stepping forward, I retreat a few steps back. There's a list a mile long of dos and don'ts involving Devon. Everyone in town has been well versed. On the flip side, I thought it was like passing out the guy's kryptonite– now everyone knows how to hurt Devon.

Rubbing at my chest, an odd sense of protectiveness descends. Dev's more vulnerable now than ever.

"We have a ton of planning to do." Essie wiggles a notebook at Beth, who pulls away from giving Devon a hug. I thought hugs were on the no list, which was fine by me, because a hug is what fucked me up in the first place. "Hope the guys don't mind if we don't help with dinner."

"I think that would be a good thing," Devon teases Essie, tugging on a piece of her hair. "Best if we keep you away from the kitchen."

"Ha-ha," Essie mock laughs, chucking Devon in the shoulder with a loosely made fist.

Tilting my head to the side, I watch as Essie and Beth treat Devon like they did years ago. No walking on eggshells, no ignoring how things have changed. As they interact, Devon relaxes more and more, and it's odd that I can sense it.

"We'll work at my desk." Beth tugs Essie across the loft. "It's not like Rory was listening to me when we were cooking anyway." Winking, Beth delivers a burn about the cheese.

"That's new," Dev points out, noticing not much but the office furnishings has changed in my bachelor pad. No matter how much I tried to avoid the guy, it was next to impossible since our lives have been intertwined. Devon helped me move in here– Auggie forced him.

"Yeah, Beth didn't have a lot of stuff." I point out how our DVD collection has grown exponentially, then to the mini office space I added to the far corner in the loft. "Hello Kitty was banned."

Devon barks a laugh, which cuts off before it reaches its natural end, like the guy is stunned the sound came out of his own mouth. "I wondered why there was random Hello Kitty paraphernalia floating around."

"It was only fitting to pawn it off on the folks at the Pink Taco Hut– lotta teenage girls." I gesture toward the kitchen, but Devon's feet don't move. I flash him a look of confusion while my nerves have me babbling. "We packed up a few boxes to give to whomever has a girl first… maybe Isis."

"We're having a boy." Devon sounds relieved not to be the recipient of the Hello Kitty curse. "Niiiiice…" he drawls out, smirking evilly. "If Isis ends up with a girl– serve Tweety right."

Snorting, I choke out, "Tweety," amused how no one but Devon can get away with calling Robin that derogatory name.

Instead of heading toward the kitchen, Devon strides a few steps toward me, and I freeze like a startled rabbit snared in the sights of a hungry fox.

Devon was confident when we were kids. He had no problem bossing me around, even though I was years older. I was down with the program, either obey or not play. But that was an empty sort of confidence. I was simultaneously relieved yet saddened to see that diminish in Devon as he grew up. Now it utterly terrifies me.

Steps faltering, Devon's confidence winks out for a split-second, only to return with a vengeance. "Test run," he murmurs underneath his breath, coming in for a hug.

Freezing, I expect the bro-hug every guy I know passes around. The lean forward, opposite shoulder touching, back pat, only lasting two seconds at the longest. As a firm body comes flush against mine, I remember who's hugging me. The guy who freaked me out– the spawn of the clingiest cop in all of Fairport.

Devon doesn't give bro-hugs. Hands hovering in the air, I'm not sure how to react. The no-no list said we had to let Devon come to us, not to initiate conversations or touch, and to always let Devon lead. The guy hesitates, as if he's tasting his own fear on the back of his tongue, then he melts into me, like he hasn't been touched in far too long.

"Thank God," Devon murmurs against my chest, shuddering. The height difference is interesting, with Dev more than a head shorter than me. He's a nice, heavy, warm weight against my chest and thighs, and he smells too goddamn good for my sanity.

Skin suddenly feeling too tight, I come to the realization that this is Devon's way of showing me how he trusts me not to harm him. Awkwardness surrounding us or not, we used to be friends eons ago.

Moving slowly, my palms land on Devon's shoulders, the pressure light enough that I barely feel him beneath my hands. We bypassed normal hugging about ten seconds ago, headed into bizarre limbo territory, and I'm not sure how to react. Let Devon lead, they said... he's not pulling away, and I don't know what to do about any of this.

"Some people I can't hug anymore, and I miss it," is Devon's odd explanation.

"Oh," I mutter lamely, at a complete and total loss. "This is nice, though." Too nice. Way too fucking nice. If my skin gets any tighter, it's going to tear.

Flesh jerks against my upper thigh, and it takes less than a heartbeat for my body to recognize it. Hopping backward, I quickly turn and make a beeline toward the kitchen, as all my blood flows southward.

History repeating itself.

Feeling like a dick, like I just rejected Devon, which is most certainly on the no-no list, I make a lame excuse. "Gotta get the chicken under the broiler." Bending down, I'm glad the heat of the oven covers my enflamed flesh. No doubt my blush is obvious, but we can at least play pretend.

"Smells good." Devon comes up behind me, then stops near the butcher block.

"Do you ever get sick of chicken?" Babbling, I get my head out of the oven, ignoring how Essie and Beth are merely pretending to plan our wedding reception. I can feel three sets of eyes boring into my flesh.

Devon releases that happy, surprised laugh, only this time he doesn't cut it off early. "Nah, I had pork the night before and fish last night. Clover keeps me fed well while I'm at work."

"Yeah, her bag-lunch service, right?" I fiddle with the green beans, deciding small talk is the way to erase the insanity of what just happened. If Devon doesn't want to acknowledge it, fine by me. "I've ordered a few cookie platters from Clover to pass out to Rush's employees during meetings."

Devon just watches me in silence, smirking knowingly. Lord knows what devious things are playing out in that wicked mind of his. When he was a little shit, he could think circles around the rest of us, like his brain was on another wavelength. We used to tease him, saying he was next year's operating system and we were Commodore 64s.

"Do you do most of the cooking?" He plays along, trying to get me to relax, and it works. The prick is infectious like a disease. More so since he returned sober and sane. There's something intriguing about Devon, where you want to please him and soak up any attention he's willing to toss your way.

"Yeah, I mean–" Puffing out my large chest, I dare Devon to call me out for not being manly. "Only child. I moved out at eighteen and had to fend for myself. I live and work here, and Beth works and goes to school around-the-clock. Only seemed fair."

Beth and I don't have traditional gender roles. That was one thing we negotiated during the flight home from Vegas. No Hello Kitty and no misogyny. We do what needs to be done when we notice it, by the right person for the job.

"I'm not–" Devon blushes bright red, which is something I've never seen before. Devon is shameless by definition. "Cooking isn't a guy versus girl thing, you get that, right?"

The girls snorting is the background track to my mortification.

"I popped out of the womb as Dad's wife and the mother figure to my future siblings." To prove a point, Devon begins gathering up things to put back in the fridge. "We all have to eat, have fresh clothes, and scrubbed toilets, right? In a house full of guys, what do we do, remain ignorant while we wait for a woman to appear out of thin air to clean after us? Weston's the best dang cleaner on the planet, and don't you dare make a gay joke– he enjoys it."

"I get it," I murmur almost inaudibly as I watch Devon like he's the most fascinating thing, all the while he shows his true anal-retentive colors– he's organizing my fridge. "I better check the chicken."

I pop back out of the oven to find Devon staring down at me. "I need to make friends who aren't related to me," he announces.

"And the pool is so small you picked me as last on your list?" The take-no-prisoners expression on Devon's face has an apology falling from my lips. "Sorry, I'm being an asshole again."

More sober than ever, "I've done things I regret. Things I cannot change. But that doesn't mean I'll do them again."

"I'm sorry," I repeat, more firmly this time. "Really. That was a low blow."

"I know I can do anything, no matter how heinous, and the girls will still love me." Devon doesn't even bother to modulate his voice so Essie and Beth won't overhear him. He also shows no remorse, because it's the honest to God's truth. "Dr. Delaney made me promise to make connections with people who aren't related to me, who won't let me bulldoze over them."

"And I qualify?" Pointing at my own chest, I'm in utter disbelief. "Did you suddenly forget how you used to bully me around when we played as kids, and I was *years* older than you?"

"You're a grown man now." Dark blue eyes rove the length of my body, and the intensity has me squirming in my boots. "I trust you to handle me."

"Handle you?" Turning quickly before Devon can see my expression, I drop the green beans into the steamer basket.

"I'm looking to buy a car," Devon announces out of nowhere.

"And your brother is a mechanic," I remind him.

"No family, remember?"

"Explain."

Chancing a glance over my shoulder, I catch sight of Devon's eyebrows knitting together in the center of his forehead. Either he's formulating a reply, or counting backward to stop himself from murdering me in my own kitchen. The jury's still out on which is the correct answer.

"Boundaries," Devon states gravely. "Because family hurt me. Family didn't protect me. Family abandoned me, or let me down, or made me take care of them when I needed to be cared for… because I hurt them, and I'm sickened over it. Because they know things about me I wish no one knew. Because family has the power to harm me, to the point I can't even hug my own goddamn dad."

"Oh, Dev," Beth and Essie's voices flow in unison across the expanse of the loft, but neither gets up to intervene. This is between Devon and me.

An ambush. They trapped me in my own home– they all know my secret.

So much for loyalty from my wife. But, then again, Tweety was there, and he's a nefarious sonofabitch. Maybe I didn't hide it so well, the reason I stopped hanging around Devon, Essie, and Beth, and started shadowing Auggie, Rob, and Isis instead. Maybe Devon always knew– maybe he felt what I felt from him during our hug.

"Dad needs to be my dad, not my friend. Ren needs to be my brother, not my friend. Auggie needs to be my uncle, not my friend. No matter if we get married and have a dozen kids, Essie will always be my best friend, as will Beth. But it's a struggle to stop myself from rolling over them, and I need you to stop me for my sake. I need friends right now, Rory– *real* friends."

Keeping my back to Devon, I whisper, "Why me?" while stirring the green beans.

"Because I miss you," whispers back softly.

"Shit," I snarl, burning my hand with a splatter of boiling water from the pot. Devon is by far better with the master of manipulation routine now that he's sober and medicated, because the sincerity would make even the most selfish assholes bend to his whim. "What kind of vehicle are you looking for?"

"Here, let me." Devon takes the spoon from my hand, shoving me out of his orbit with his hip. He's glowing with a high from making me do something I already wanted to do but was too stubborn to admit it. "With the kid coming, I know I should get something safe and reliable."

A retching sound comes from my chest. "You're a man. Men drive machines, not cars."

"Lord, save us!" Beth prays dramatically, hands flying up into the air. "Rory dreams about his *car* in his sleep."

"She's not a car– she's a machine." Insulted on behalf of my Dodge Challenger, I glare at my wife. "Devon understands, because he grew up with the Pussy Magnet."

"Kyle took me out today, and he wanted me to buy a Subaru." We share a shudder. "The responsible thing to do would be to buy two cheap, reliable cars, knowing Ren could fix whatever breaks, so Essie would have wheels too."

"God, no," I mutter in horror. "Don't do that– never."

"Yeah, well…" Devon lifts the steamer basket out of the boiling water, then dumps the green beans in a bowl. "I may not have any choice in the matter. Ren has his truck. Willow's using Rob's old Explorer–"

"And she won't share," comes from multiple sources, including me.

Devon releases that carefree laugh again, and we all look at him like he's emitting goddamn sunshine from his vocal cords.

"Willow keeps going on and on about buying a truck with a ladder rack like Uncle Dave's." Essie's voice has a teasing note, evidently finding Willow's bad behavior adorable. "If you buy a new car, Willow's keeping-up-with-the-Joneses attitude will have her buying a truck quick as shit, and I'll inherit the Explorer."

"I love your devious mind," comes from the most devious. "I just can't do a van or sedan. Ugh."

"Let's table this while we get the food on the table," I mutter while bending to check out the chicken under the broiler. "Looks done."

Working as a four-person team, the table is covered in food it took me all day to prepare, with spoons and forks loading plates to max-capacity. "This looks really good," Essie purrs, gazing at her plate like a man does pornography. "This baby loves to eat."

"Pregnancy looks good on you." I flash a smile in Essie's direction, compliment not bullshit. The woman looks absolutely stunning, and it's taken everything in me not to bury my face in her tits. The farther along she gets, the more she glows. Or it could be because Devon's been home for three days, and things seem to be going nicely.

"Thanks." Eyes closed in a dreamy expression, Essie savors a bite of pasta salad. "There's a stigma about pregnant ladies, like we suddenly turned into these creatures who want people to touch our bellies, our sexuality evaporated, and we're fat and miserable."

"Idiots," Beth snarls. "And don't fret about how much weight you have to lose after the baby is born. I know better than most how size has nothing to do with sexual gratification. Some of the thinnest women in the Playroom had major sexual hang-ups. The older, voluptuous ladies pitched their insecurities years ago, and it showed in how satisfied their lovers were."

My wife is a bigger girl, bound to get curvier as she ages, judging by my mother-in-law's shape. I'm a blissed out man, and my wife knows it. I have no idea what Devon's preferences are, but Essie will always be sexy as fuck, no matter what size she is.

Both girls made me horny when I was too young, and now my pants are getting tight just sitting here watching them eat the dinner I prepared. Best change the subject before my body takes on a mind of its own and I do something stupid.

"Does it suck not being able to eat food you crave?" As soon as the words are out of my mouth, I regret them. "Shit, I'm sorry. That was rude as all get out."

"Nah, it's alright." Devon touches my hand lightly with a fingertip, then goes back to rubbing the handle to his fork. I've noticed the tics over the past few days, and it reminded me of when we were younger, how he'd touch things differently than most kids. Right now, he's rubbing his fork instead of eating with it.

"My sensitive stomach isn't from the damage I caused with the drugs." If Devon speaks, he doesn't eat, and that worries me. "I spent a long time going up and down, eating only to stay alive. It's not something I see as enjoyment, not now or back then. The healthy food and the schedule is to ensure I get enough nutrients to fuel my body, and my meds give me an upset stomach."

"So you don't crave pizza or burgers?" Baffled, I try to imagine living in a world where I didn't want treats. "I got you an angel food cake, is that okay for you to eat?"

Devon releases that laugh again, and I can't hide the shudder that works its way along my spine to light in my nuts. "It's just egg whites and sugar– Clover taught us how to make it a few months ago, and it's one of the desserts I can eat nonstop without getting sick… chocolate cake is another story, best not told while eating."

Beth and Essie join Devon, laughing over an inside joke I don't understand. "Clover made me pizza with a gluten-free cauliflower crust, but I couldn't eat it. Colin let me eat half a slice of real pizza with no toppings, and I was good with just a few bites."

"You didn't get sick?" Essie asks, surprised.

"Nope," Devon pops the P, then takes a bite of salad, avoiding the cheese. "I can practically read your mind, Rory. I derive no real pleasure from food. I'm terrified to hug my family, so no comfort on that end. I can't take drugs or alcohol for the rest of my life. I have to avoid over-the-counter and prescription meds."

Gobsmacked, I just gape at Devon with my mouth hanging open, fork hovering in midair.

"What joy do I have in life, right?" Devon levels me with a look so potent I'm rendered immobile. Suddenly hot, I can't even squirm in my seat. Leaning toward me, that finger's no longer caressing his fork– my wrist catches fire. "Sex."

"What?" blurts out my numb lips.

"Sex," Devon purrs in a voice gone husky with lust. "Sex is a natural high." Pleased with himself for turning my mind to mush, Devon takes three big bites of the food I prepared, all the while Essie, Beth, and I stare back at him. "It's about trust, because you have to let go enough to lose control to get off. That's why…" he trails off, speaking directly to Essie about something I'll never understand.

"That makes complete sense," my psychology major wife jumps into the conversation. "Dev, you're probably always keeping firm control over your emotions, your body, even your mind. It must be hard to let go when you're worried you won't be able to regain your control once you come down from the high."

"Exactly." Devon replies to my wife but he's looking at me.

Beth and I talked about Devon last night, and she feared his meds would affect his ability to either get hard or get off. I told her how I'd hate to be Devon, not enjoying food, or a drink, or a smoke, never being able to just let go. He was a horny fucker as a kid, but showed no interest for years, which was a relief for me. But I guess that's not an issue anymore, since I felt *him* earlier during our hug.

"So I can live without everything else, as long as I can escape into amazing sex." Devon's eyes skate from one set of eyes to the next, like he has a secret, and I'm the only one who's out of the loop. "I struggled a long time with the one man, one woman mentality. I felt like I cheated on Essie with other people, even though we weren't together. Let's just say, when I had to give up hardcore drugs…" Devon shudders, pain crossing his features. "I opened my mind to other possibilities."

"Being in the Playroom probably helped, didn't it?" I ask to shift the conversation since everyone is staring at me for some reason I refuse to contemplate. "I was always too freaked out to go in there. Place seemed to cause more pain than pleasure."

Beth looks at me, eyebrow raised, knowing damned well I refused to enter because my secret would have exploded out of me in a rush. For three days, Beth's looked at me like she's never met me before, and who she sees is a miserable fuck who lies to himself.

"Yeah." Devon's gaze shifts to Beth's and holds for several suspended seconds. "I didn't want to admit I belonged in the Playroom– Ren didn't, though. He liked it in there because he's a guy, but he didn't need it."

"Yeah, well…" Essie's voice breaks. "I was terrified the two times I snuck in there, but it was all about Willow and nothing more." Face warping with rage, "My cousin should've never set foot in there. I don't care what consenting adults do, but she wasn't an adult in my eyes."

"What about the attic?" Devon's question holds more weight than it appears, like the answer matters.

"The attic was awesome." Essie's face brightens, like she's reliving a memory. "But not if a bunch of people are in there. It's about trust, like you said. I don't exactly have a good track record in the sex department."

Tears spring to Bethany's eyes and she reaches across the table to comfort her friend. I respect them both by not demanding to know what that's about. "You know, maybe only give blowjobs to people you love, trust, and want, girlfriend. As for sex, there are people who would never hurt you, who want you as much as you want them."

Sharing a look, the girls break out into a giggle fit, with Devon smirking fondly. Meanwhile, I'm left out of the loop as always.

Just like this trap of a dinner party, I begin to wonder if this conversation was also pre-arranged. Beth's been acting squirrely since my breakdown, bringing up conversations about me exploring my sexuality. I told her I couldn't fathom a woman on the planet who would give up monogamy, and she schooled me how it wasn't synonymous with fidelity. The conversation twisted me in knots, where I began to wonder if Beth was okay with just screwing me for life, which spawned a different conversation entirely.

"I was thinking something small," Essie's voice filters into my inner turmoil. "Maybe in the backyard. We could just have Mayor Ross marry us, since Devon's an atheist."

Oh, so the girls weren't just planning Beth's and my reception.

"Congratulations," I mutter lamely, with only Devon hearing. He smirks in response, reading me better than Beth does. Embarrassed, I clear my throat a few times. "So, when do you want to check out vehicles?"

"I think Ross is a great idea– the old coot is a hoot." Beth's glowing vibrantly, happy to have her best friends near her, both of them happy and healthy after nearly a decade of intense pain. "But not the backyard. C'mon, we can come up with something better than that."

Mouth open, Devon realizes anything he says will be drowned out by two women in the midst of an intense wedding planning session. Tipping his chin in the direction of the kitchen, he gets up from the table, and I follow.

"Doesn't seem fair we have to clean up if we cooked," Devon says loudly, voice projecting. If it registers in with the girls, they don't respond. "Whoever cooked, always got first dibs on the bathroom, and got to watch TV while the rest of us cleaned up. That's the rules."

"I like those rules," rolls easily off my tongue as I begin loading the dishwasher. "Beth chains me in the kitchen."

"I. Do. Not." squawks loudly, proving the girls are listening, no matter how much verbal vomit is spilling out of their mouths. "Hydrangeas are beautiful. What about colors? That would be the best place to start."

"Thank God," Devon groans, stretching. Arms reaching toward the ceiling, his t-shirt rides up, showing off cut abs and a dark happy trail headed south. He's thin– too thin, but healthy. Every muscle is visible through his tan flesh, with his hip bones peeking out the top of his cotton shorts. The farther he stretches, the more his bulge thrusts forward.

Blinking, my eyes flick away quickly. After my momentary insanity, I pluck a few plates off the counter to scrape off into the trashcan. "Thank God?"

"Thank God, they have each other." Devon visibly shudders. "I'd shoot myself in the head if I had to listen to that nonstop– I could give a shit less." He takes in my appalled expression. "What? If anyone can make suicide jokes, it's me."

"Point taken." It's a relief to see Devon's as dark as he used to be. The medication doesn't seem to be altering his personality. Wish it would change some things, though. "I'm helping plan my own reception."

Back bristling up, ever since I admitted what I am, I feel like I have a target on my back for not being straight. Like being the domesticated one in our marriage, or someone who likes to plan parties and socializes, automatically makes me a girl.

Devon just stares at me, silently calling me out on my bullshit, like he can read my mind. "We're two men talking about cars, while our wives plan parties– it doesn't get any more masculine than that." He gets right to the heart of the matter. "Getting a stiffy while hugging another dude– nothing's more masculine than that."

"I–"

"Two dicks, ya know? The very definition of being a dude. Who said it was best to be masculine and worse to be feminine? Why is that an insult? It's ridiculous." Devon squints like he's warring inside his brain. "Beth and I had a little chat last night," he warns, or maybe it's a threat of what's to come. "Your malfunction was never one I had... I'm a man, inside and out, and it doesn't matter what happens to me, or what I do, or who I fuck, I'm still going to be a man. I've heard it all after being so short, but there isn't a cell in my body that isn't male. It's who I am, but that doesn't make being a girl less."

"Um… point taken." Blushing, I quickly fill the dishwasher while Devon shoves leftovers into the fridge.

"Guilt?" Devon's laughter isn't the bright, magnetic sound as before. It hits my ears and stings the back of my eyes. "Guilt will be buried beside me in the coffin next to addiction– no escaping it."

"Yeah, I've been suffering with a hefty dose of that too." Devon grunts in reply, and I begin to wonder what else Bethany said to Devon during their chat last night. "So what's the plan about vehicle shopping? I have to man the door by eight tomorrow night, and I'm busy until noon doing clerical bullshit."

"My shift ends at four." Devon dries his hands on a dishrag, making himself at home. The fact that his family owns this place is something he never let me forget. But I always knew Devon was punishing me for ignoring him. "Ozzy's been picking my ass up in the Pussy Magnet. So just come get me from the Batcave, and we can hit the dealerships."

"Okay, sounds good," I mutter absentmindedly as I glance at the clock. "I have to be downstairs in a few minutes."

"I'll walk you out." Devon tosses my dishrag into the sink, acting like this is his apartment and I'm his guest. "Take a break before I give my two-cents on the wedding preparations."

Stealing a kiss from my wife, Beth can barely kiss me back she's laughing so hard. I muss Essie's hair up on my way by, checking out her assets as I go.

The Devon I used to know was a possessive asshole who would've dropkicked me for staring at Essie's tits. Something major shifted in him. I was never the possessive type, especially after learning who Beth is at her core. Hard to be possessive of a girl who loves delving into people's psyches and honestly believes they're not fucked up for wanting what they want.

Stepping out into the hallway, with the closed door at my back, Devon stops me with a palm pressed to my chest.

"I meant what I said." The guy reads my mind again, and it's unnerving as all hell. "It's not that I'm wired differently than before– it's that I finally accepted that I am. Go ahead and look at Essie's tits. Lord knows, Ren's still jerking off over 'em."

"I'm not gonna lie, being around Beth and Auggie at the same time is difficult for me. They look at each other too intimately, and it rubs me raw. After Auggie did what he did to me... I wonder if Beth feels the same way. So I'll try not to look at Essie's chest again."

"I used to stalk and arrest anyone Essie touched– I tried to kill Ren in his sleep." Devon arches a brow in my direction, lips curled sinisterly. "Dr. Delaney and Ms. Amelia forced me to grow the fuck up. Now I register how you're looking at Essie like you appreciate her, not just want to use her up and toss her away– that was the sex comment Beth made earlier. Essie and I have a lot in common."

"Shit." Wincing, I try not to think too deeply on what Dev's admitting, because it turns my guts. "You guys ambushed me tonight, didn't you?"

"I didn't," Dev admits, and I can tell it's the truth. "Can't comment on the girls, though. They're always scheming something."

"Well, I'll see you at four tomorrow afternoon." Stepping to the side, I force Devon to drop his hand from my chest. "Get a good idea on how much you're willing to finance and what type of vehicle you want."

"Wait!" The warm palm is back, rooted in place like it belongs there. "Are we good?"

"Yeah, why?"

"Because I treated you like shit, but I can't apologize because it won't change the past," Devon blurts out quickly, fearful I won't let him speak his piece.

"I treated you like shit too, remember?"

"Yeah, but... see, now I understand why people do and say the things they do, so I don't blame them. I'm a difficult person to be around– I get that. So I just want to know if we're good or not, because I want us to be friends again."

"Why?" I breathe softly, more than curious as to why Dev's had a sudden change of heart.

"I was jealous that you picked my aunt and uncle and Robin to hang around, not gonna lie. So I acted like the biggest fuckhead on the planet. Not *acted*, I was a fuckhead. Still am, I just control myself better." Taking a deep breath, "We good?"

"We're good," falls off my tongue before I can stop it, because Devon's in sincerity manipulation mode and I'm too weak to resist it. Staring down at his hand, I decide to bite the bullet and just ask. "What's with the hug and the touching?"

Blushing, Devon looks away, but he doesn't drop his hand. "Did Beth tell you about why I didn't want people hugging me?"

"Yeah, but... she didn't go into detail," I stammer, getting tongue-tied over the subject. There was gossip making its rounds for years, but I was never sure how much it was seeded in truth. Now I know, and I wished I didn't.

"Subconsciously, I resent my dad, so I don't want him to touch me. It's raw, like it just happened a few months ago, not seven years ago. Big guys intimidate me– *he was big*," Devon whispers, pain lacing his words. "But you... you make me feel safe, so I want to be your friend."

"I make you feel safe?" I repeat like an idiot. "But I'm a huge guy."

"Yeah, you make me feel safe because I trust you and you're big enough to stop me. You won't put up with my shit, because it'll hurt Bethany and Essie." Hopeful in his manipulations, Devon looks a question at me.

Curiosity gets the better of me, but it's the anticipation that's driving me. "What does being your friend entail exactly?"

"Just..." Devon shrugs, looking at a loss for words. "I don't know, to be honest."

Closing my eyes, I war with myself. "A hug?" I realize it doesn't matter, since the truth is already out there. If I get hard, I do. So what? It's not like Dev's a hyper-sexualized kid and I'm a late bloomer too weak to not be drawn into his flirty swagger.

"I could use a hug." As Devon gulps audibly, I watch his throat move. "It's incomprehensible, wanting something that terrifies me. I crave hugs more than I crave drugs. They simultaneously make me feel safe yet terrified, and it opens me up to feel things I'd rather didn't exist."

"Since you've been home, who's given you the best hug?" Leaning against the wall, I try to look relaxed and at ease.

"Rob," Devon admits without hesitation. "Not because it was comforting or safe, but because it was challenging. He gave me more clarity than dozens of psychologists did over the past seven years."

"Challenging, that's our Robin Prynne," I muse, surprised over Devon's choice. "Clarity in what?"

"Clarity in what I need." Devon steps against my chest, hesitating, testing his resolve, tasting his own fear. "And to not feel guilty or the need to apologize for it."

"Oh–" a tight body presses against mine, arms wrapping around my back, beneath mine. Bethany warned how Devon freaks out if his arms are pinned during a hug, which is why he hugs everyone else, arms always on top. Yet he purposefully pins himself against me.

Just as before, Devon freezes for a few seconds, then melts into my body. This isn't like a hug I've ever experienced. It's no different than holding a lover in bed, yet we're standing up against the wall. Head resting against my chest, with his chest pressed against my belly, we're connected all the way to our feet.

After a moment's hesitation, I test a theory. Arms wrapping around Devon's back, I squeeze tightly. The harder I squeeze, the more Devon relaxes. Sighing deeply, the guy's eyelashes flutter like he just took a hefty toke of smoke.

There's no rubbing or patting hands. We're just standing woven together tightly in a level of intimacy I thought impossible to feel with a friend. It's not romantic in nature, but there's most definitely a sexual edge. It doesn't matter the gender, a person would have to be dead to not want Devon Mason writhing under or above them.

Time stills as I rest my cheek against the top of Devon's head, our bodies pressed together, hard-ons ignored but not forgotten. After a long while, he steps back, looking like a guy who's been hardcore fucked into oblivion while chasing his favorite vices.

"You're late for work." Devon blushes, stepping away to reach for the doorknob to the apartment door. "Sorry."

"It's alright," I slur, blinking. "One of the benefits of being the manager– I'll see you at four tomorrow."

"Night," Devon whispers, slinking back into my apartment like he owns the place.

In a daze, I quickly skip down the steps, then waltz down the hallway to the club proper, swaying slightly as if I've been drinking. My bartender meets me halfway to the bar. "You're late," Carrie teases. "What's up with you? You're all flushed."

"I feel good, is all," I slur on my way by, making my way to the front door. "It's a good thing it's Tuesday night," I speak over my shoulder to Carrie.

"Yeah, I didn't have to card many people." She reassures me as she steps back behind the bar. "You sure you're okay? You look fucking high."

"I'm good." Blinking repeatedly, I shake my head left and right. "Damn good."

CHAPTER THREE

"What are you working on?" Having time to kill before I have to pick Devon up in the Courthouse basement, I pester my wife. Resting my hip on the edge of her desk, I try to spy on her work.

"A case study on incest." Bethany moves to the side, giving me total access to her laptop, trusting me infallibly.

"You have access to a case study on *that*." Eyes bugging out of my head, I'm more than impressed by my wife.

"Nope." Bethany grins up at me. "I'm *writing* a case study on that."

"Holy shit, little pup." Awed, my pride in Bethany quadruples in mere seconds. "Why do you only have an **L** and **P** where their names should be?"

"*Incest*," she stresses, parting her hands in a '*there you go*' motion. "Plus, I hope to publish it at some point in my career."

"Wow... how did you find them? How do you contact them?" I've always taken an interest in everything Bethany does, but this is one helluva topic that I can't leave alone. "If you're chatting with them, they must be here in Fairport."

"Skype." Beth's eyes are filled with silent laughter– laughing at my obvious ass. There's a reason I get along so well with both Robin and Essie. I love to gossip too. "Let's just say this case study is connected to another I'm working on, so I just followed the breadcrumbs to **L** and **P**. Their story is tragic but also inspiring."

"Incest is inspiring?" Leaning forward, I read a paragraph before Bethany clicks a button on her laptop, covering the document with her Facebook newsfeed. Narrowing my eyes, a political meme fills my vision.

"It's not ready for anyone but me to read just yet. I have to make sure there are no identifying details," Beth cautions, because I'm breaking her rules of ethics. "Tragic because their story is based on everlasting love. Imagine falling in love, sharing your body, finding out you're going to be parents, so you bring your partner to visit your parents."

"Sounds like everybody's love story." Shifting on the desk, I cross my arms over my chest. "What happens next?" I wait for the tragic punchline.

"Your mother faints and your father calls you a sinful abomination for fucking a brother you didn't know you had–"

"What the…" Drawing in a deep breath, I can't even contemplate how that would feel.

"It's life-destroying for all involved, especially for the baby. Imagine the cross the child would have to bear as they go through life."

"For the love of all that's holy, get to the inspiring part of this wicked story."

"Wicked?" Bethany snorts, finger flashing out to press a button on her keyboard. The title of her case study flashes on the screen. **WICKED**. "The inspiring part is how **L** and **P** found acceptance by forgiving themselves for sins they didn't realize they committed. They weren't at fault, and they shouldn't have to suffer the consequences for their parents' actions. Their children…"

"Are still waiting for their inspiration?" I guess. "Wait! What? You said *children*."

"One created out of innocence and one during sin. Both incredible, worthy human beings who belong on this earth." Empathetic in the extreme, Beth brushes a few stray tears from her eyes. "Now that's inspiring."

"Yeah, I don't know where to take our conversation from there," I mumble, heart hurting because I'm not a moron. I know exactly where Bethany's breadcrumb trail leads, and no way am I cleaning that shit off my doorstep. "I guess I better go pick up Dev."

"Don't sound so put out," Bethany teases me, fingernail trailing along my arm. "I can tell you're nervous yet excited about your friendship date."

"Friendship date?" Head whipping to the side, I'm not sure I heard her right. "What the fuck, Beth?"

"Friendship date– your second one with Devon." Beth smirks at me knowingly. "Last night was your first date."

"I repeat. What. The. Actual. Fuck?"

"There is nothing Essie and I don't share."

My wife's words have me choking for several reasons, but mostly for what isn't being implied but shoved in my face. "Oh, yeah? Is that why you're both working overtime to get your husbands laid… with each other?"

Blushing, looking flustered, "That's not what I mean, dammit!" Scrubbing at her face with upraised palms, if I wasn't so pissed at Beth, I'd think she looked adorable. "Everyone on this planet needs one friend that belongs to them."

"I thought you said possessiveness was for narrow-minded control-freaks and abusive partners?" I remind my wife of the dozens of conversations we've had on this subject.

"Not like that, dipshit!"

"Ugh!" Head cranking back sharply, Bethany palms my forehead and shoves to get me to shut up and let her speak. "Speaking of spousal abuse…"

"Just listen, okay?" Smirking, I make the universal zip my lips and twist a key motion. "Good," Bethany murmurs calmly, face still blazing with a crimson kiss. "Everyone needs someone who is just theirs. I can go to Essie for anything, and I mean *anything*. If I had a body to hide, she'd be my go-to girl."

"Not me? I'm strong enough to carry the heaviest of men." Popping an eyebrow, I try my damnedest not to smirk. "Never mind– it's probably my body you're burying anyway."

"Ha-ha." Beth sticks her tongue out at me. "But you're finally getting the point. We live in reality, where people bitch about their spouses, knowing it's not always going to be sunshine and rainbows day in and day out. It's going to be work, and we all need a friend to either let us bitch, or bawl on their shoulder, or tell us we're being unreasonable."

"Let me get this straight…" I pin my wife with a glare. "You and your bestie picked me and Devon out a bestie… each other. So, while yours will help you bury a body, you gave me the prick who will most likely premeditatedly murder someone when he goes off his meds, and I'll be the idiot holding a shovel and a bloody shower curtain."

"As long as you're not burying Essie, I'm good with that." Beth manages to say with a straight face. "But, yeah, you're getting the gist."

"You didn't think me capable of picking out my own partner in crime?" I sound more than vaguely insulted.

"Actually?" Beth holds my gaze unflinchingly. "No. You never made friends your own age. When we moved across the street from each other, you were automatically friends with my friends. But we all knew they were mine. So then you ended up with the deviant trio, but we all know they put each other first."

"Thanks," I mutter dryly, pissed the fuck off.

"But we're not kids anymore– we're all the same age, in the same stage in life. Essie and I have each other. The deviant trio is tearing each other to shreds, and you don't want their shit on your doorstep anymore. That leaves you and Devon, two people who do have a lot in common–"

"You and Essie," I point out, but Beth ignores me, still selling me on Devon.

"You enjoy each other's company. You used to be friends, but both of you were too obsessed with Essie and me to truly get to know each other. Without us in the way, with Devon being all enlightened and you admitting what you want, Essie and I think you guys could be just as close as we are."

"Except you don't want to fuck Essie." Lunging from the desk, the words are out of my mouth before I can stop them.

Laughing with sheer relief, "Oh. My. God! You finally fucking admitted it! *I knew it*. That's why you blew us off, wasn't it? It's why you wouldn't hang out with us anymore? Devon was a horny little bastard, that's for damn sure."

"Shut it!" I warn, not in the mood to be teased. "It's true, though. Sex won't get in between your relationship with Essie."

"You say that as if Essie and I haven't gotten each other off before," my wife mutters wryly.

Hand flying to cup my bulge, I suck back several large breaths as I try to control my involuntary body functions. A wet spot grows beneath my palm, mortifying me beyond belief.

"It's not the same as you and Dev, I will admit." Beth ignores the horrified expression on my face, and the filthy condition I'm in. "I'll do anything for Essie. *Anything*. Sex has fucked with her head and made her feel horrible about herself. Dev still has some serious issues." Beth stares me down. *"Anything."*

"Do you hear yourself?" Stalking across the loft, I fling the fridge door open, reaching in for a beer. Then I remember I'm meeting Devon, and I won't be a selfish bastard by showing up with beer breath. "You're pimping out your own husband. Don't you see that as cheating?"

"Pimping out my husband?" Beth laughs, and there isn't a single note of anger or resentment lacing it. Just pure amusement. "You were out in the hallway for over an hour, holding each other, dumbass. No matter what level of education I achieve, two plus two will always equal four."

"It wasn't just a hug," I stress. "I've felt guilty as fuck since the high wore off."

"Don't," Beth pleads with me. "Never feel guilty for your true emotions."

"We're guys– that intensity of intimacy leads to sex. Don't you get that?"

"So?" Beth has the audacity to say.

"So?!" I bellow, emotions pinging all over the place. "You'd be okay if I fucked Devon?"

"Your nutsack emptied when I insinuated I'd touched Essie before," Beth mutters pointedly, eyes boring into my damp crotch. "If you fucked some random person, I'd cut off said nuts. If you end up touching Devon, I'd probably get off on just the thought of it too. That is the difference."

"Really?" Baffled, all I can do is stare at my wife in utter disbelief.

"Really." Beth wiggles around in her chair, as if the thought alone is getting her hot. "If you guys picked up a hooker, Essie and I would be disposing of a bloody shower curtain and a shovel. But if it's just two friends–"

"You're insane!"

"There is a difference between monogamy and fidelity. They are not mutually exclusive. If I threw Essie on the table in the middle of dinner and decided to eat her instead, you and Devon would probably bust a nut. Don't you think that perhaps the reverse would hold true for Essie and me?"

"Jesus." Panting heavily, I reach down to adjust my junk. "Please stop this insanity."

"Rory." Beth approaches me slowly, which signals I'm not imagining the tears of terror in my eyes. "I don't want you to wake up one day, when you're fifty, resenting the fact that you've denied your sexuality and you regret not experiencing your true nature."

"I love you!" I cry out, terrified I'll lose my wife to this insanity. "I want you so fucking much. Your body drives me insane. I love everything about you."

"And I love you so much, I won't stifle you. I trust us. *Us*. I trust our love. I trust our fidelity. I trust we will never do anything to the other to purposefully cause harm. I don't have to live by society's standards of love to prove it." Beth points at her laptop and the case study on the screen. "We only have one life to live, with no do-overs. I'm not going to push you in a tiny box, force you to live by standards that aren't your own, and call what is tantamount to abuse love."

"I–"

"We live in reality. Being in love and getting married does not mean I cut your balls off and stuff them in my purse, only to retrieve them when I want to get fucked or knocked up. It doesn't mean we suddenly stop finding other people attractive, sexually or otherwise. To believe that hogwash is to buy into an unobtainable fantasy that will lead to an abuse of power in the relationship, and ultimately a divorce. I love you, Rory. Not the idea of you. Not the form I want to shape you into. *You*."

"I find it hard to believe you'd be okay with this– I don't know if I'm okay with this, or if I'm feeling off because I don't think I should be okay with this, but I am. A manly man would probably be running off to fuck Devon right now, but I feel bad about myself for stopping to think it through. But you– you're good with it."

"*You* wanting *Devon* is not about *me*. Possessiveness is not flattering. It's abusive. It's controlling. It's for the sake of ego to cover deep-seated insecurities. I'm not any of those things, and neither are you. I just want you to be happy, Rory."

"I am," I deny, voice wavering.

"No, you're not," Beth stresses, seeing right through me. "You're my husband, and you're everything I need in a partner. But one person cannot complete another. I need Essie. I need my parents. I need our other friends. I need my future clients to feel worthy. You need those things too– people outside of me. Someone who gets you, when I can't because it's about me."

Beth reaches out to me, drawing me down to the sofa. "Babe?" She brushes stray tears off my cheeks. "It's not healthy to put everything into one person. This is life, and it isn't infinite. I could survive losing Essie if I still had you to support me–"

"But what am *I* going to do if I lose you?" Heart beating a wicked tattoo in my chest, terror has adrenaline flooding my veins. "Can we at least have our wedding reception before we're worried about being widowed, please?"

Laughing lightly, Beth squeezes me tightly. "You married a woman who gets off on fiddling inside people's heads, Rory. I see the complexity in emotions others see as simple."

"You're saying I need a life– Devon needs a life?"

"Yeah, I am. I'm not going to cheat on Essie by spending too much time with you," Beth teases, voice holding amusement. "Besides, we'd get sick of each other. Expand your horizons outside of this building." Pushing me off the sofa, "Go on your friendship date."

"But…" Pausing, feet refusing to move, I glance down at my wife. "What if our next hug goes too far?"

"Boundaries?" Beth guesses. "I have divided loyalties, Rory. I don't want to have any secrets from you or Essie. Essie doesn't want to have any secrets from Devon or me. It would be easier if you and Dev would get there too, so none of us has to fear saying too much and betraying someone by accident."

Standing from the sofa, Beth strides across the loft to our bedroom area, then pulls open my drawer in the dresser. "Fidelity. It's not cheating if you're with Devon, or I'm with Essie, in any capacity. I'm not a fool, babe. Essie's hot as fuck, so if you ever touch her, we all have to be present."

"Oh, my God." Grabbing at my package, I'm beginning to think I've entered an alternate universe. "You're joking, right?"

"No, I'm not." Beth tosses a fresh pair of boxers at me, with a pair of jeans following in their wake. "I told you Essie has a horrible sexual history, one too close to Devon's to make them compatible right now. You're a gentle lover, and Devon's not."

Getting a clue, "You want to fuck Devon?"

"And you don't?" Completely unrepentant, Bethany grins at me. "It's not on my to-do list, but I wouldn't turn the guy down. You know me and intensity. Something tells me the guy would probably burn the earth to the ground when he gets off. I'm sure you'll find out sooner than I will."

"Sometimes I forget who you are and where you've been," I mumble in a daze. "The little girl with sidewalk chalk staining her fingertips pink thrived in the Playroom and is specializing in human sexuality."

"Redress," Beth orders, palm cupping my crotch. Grunting, I can't help but thrust forward into her hand. "Devon deserves better than you showing up with spunk leaking through your pants– you're going to be late."

"We're just getting a new vehicle," I remind Beth as I drop trou.

"And you're a car guy, so spiffy up for the new lady you pick out," Beth teases me, all the while watching me with an appreciative eye as I tug on a fresh pair of jeans.

"Devon's straight," spills out of my lips as I zip up. "He's not going to have sex with me."

"Is he?" Beth looks at me with her head cocked to the side. "This friendship shit would be easier if we were *all* in it together," she stresses. "And, no, he's not going to have sex with you tonight. It's only your second date– Dev doesn't put out easily."

"You're making fun of me, I just know it." Swaggering forward, I cup the back of Beth's neck, drawing her lips to mine. "If it's intensity you want, I'm going to fuck you into the mattress when I get home," I warn, meaning it.

Pupils blown, Beth stares up at me through the fringe of her lashes, lips moistened from my kiss. "I'll be ready and waiting," she murmurs in a voice gone husky with lust. "Make it hard. Make it hurt. Make it so I'm still feeling you next week."

CHAPTER FOUR

Avoiding Malcolm Mason on purpose, I stalk by his second-in-command's desk instead. "Hey, Colin!" Raising my hand in a wave, I don't feel freaked out at all. Not at all. "Hey, Kyle. How's it hanging?"

"To the left," the cop teases me, hitching up a pant leg before falling into the chair at his desk.

I should befriend Kyle. The sweet guy is safe, sane, and I'm more likely to be sexually attracted to my grandmother than him. Beth really likes Kyle's wife, Renée.

"You graduated together, Rory," Bethany's voice flows inside my head. *"If you were meant to be friends, you had twelve years of opportunities."*

"I'm looking for Devon." Voice cracking with nerves, I flinch. "Have you seen him around?"

"Just took off to hit the head, I think," Kyle mutters absentmindedly, reaching for a file on his desk.

"Thanks." I weave past his desk. "I could take a leak myself." Taking a wild guess, I head in the direction of the lighted restroom sign. There's probably a locker room hidden in the dark depths of this underground bunker, but most men would just piss in the closest toilet.

Walking through the swinging door, my steps falter as Devon's gaze connects with mine in the reflection of the mirror. Playing pretend, I stalk up to the urinal next to his, knowing I'd look like an ass if I took the one farthest away from him.

"I wasn't sure if you'd show." Devon breaks urinal etiquette by chatting with me while we take a piss. My zipper sounds louder than a gunshot.

Jumping, my dick is extra-sensitive as I pull it free from my fly. "We're shopping for a machine– I wouldn't miss that for anything in the world."

Awkwardness descends. Do we keep chatting to cover the sound of our piss hitting the porcelain, or do we just ignore each other until we jiggle our dicks free of drips?

Unbidden, I break the cardinal rule. My eyes flick downward just as Devon starts to tuck himself away. It's only for less than a split-second, but he must have felt my eyes light on his dick.

Upping his game, the intense motherfucker turns to the side and stares at my dick. Have you ever tried to take a piss while being watched? Have you ever tried to take a piss and stop mid-stream? Have you ever had to do all these things while all the blood in your body flows south?

One Mississippi.

Two Mississippi.

Three Mississippi.

"You have a big dick," the sadist comments conversationally, eyes never leaving my flesh. "Thick and meaty."

Yeah, that's how you stop peeing mid-stream by getting a hard-on.

"You're a creepy motherfucker," is the only reply I can come up with.

"I keep saying it, but no one listens. Sober and medicated does not mean I had a personality transplant." Devon actually pats me on the back as I struggle to shove my hard dick back into my pants. "I'm trying to be good, but–"

"I'm such an easy target?" Thank fuck, my zipper didn't get stuck.

"Here's my apology," Devon deadpans, grabbing for my hand. Next thing I know, my palm is cupping a compact bulge hard enough to pound nails. "I wasn't jerking your chain– I was giving you a compliment."

"Jesus fuck." Hissing through my front teeth, I'm at a complete and total loss. "This doesn't seem like friendship behavior."

"Still me." Devon chuckles sinisterly. "Can I have my hug now?"

"Are you–" *Insane.* Eyes flicking around, I realize anyone could walk in at any time, and we're just metaphorically standing around with our hard dicks in our hands. Tugging Devon into the closest stall, I lock us in. "Are you shitting me? For real? You're making my head spin."

"No one has ever accused me of being boring." Devon of the no vices, he's toying with me. "You asked me how I have the will to live without being able to eat, or drink, or do drugs, or lose control–"

"I didn't ask you that," I furiously whisper back.

"Well, you thought it," Devon challenges me, eyes boring into mine. "I'm having fun with you."

"At my expense," I snarl, crossing my arms over my chest.

"Lighten up, Rory." Devon has the audacity to skate a single fingertip over the outline of my hard-on. Shivering, it takes everything in me not to buck up into his touch. "I've been through some devastating shit. Watching you get hard while taking a piss, that was a highlight, not a tragedy."

"You're creepy."

"When have I not been?" Devon volleys back at me. "I only allow some people to know the real me. Most wouldn't understand."

"Motherfucker." Sighing, I stare at the ceiling, wondering if I'll ever be immune to this bastard's manipulations. "Fine." I part my arms. "Get over here and get it over with."

"You act like you don't enjoy it as much as me." Dev has my goddamn number. "I tried to get you to hug me when we were younger, but you flipped out on me because you liked it."

This time, there's no hesitation, no freezing, no testing of his resolve. Devon melts into me on contact, sighing contentedly while pressing every inch of his body against mine. "This feels good– safe."

I refuse to comment on that, but my arms squeeze tighter, body arcing with his. "Has your future wife been saying to you what mine has been saying to me?"

Devon's snort vibrates against my chest. "Did you forget what it's like to be tag-teamed by them?" Even without sexual connotations, I'm shuddering at the thought. "What do you think they talked about while you were at work last night? There was no wedding planning done in my presence."

"You're shitting me, right?" Pulling away, I gaze down at Devon.

"Bethany and I speak the same language after our stint in the Playroom. So basically we were explaining the finer points to Essie– nothing else, nothing more."

"Oh," I grunt, relieved. "Good."

The sound of the bathroom door opening has us clinging tighter together instead of jumping apart. "Son?" Malcom Mason's voice has my dick shrinking down in a nanosecond. "You okay in there."

"Go away, Dad." Devon's voice takes on a note I haven't heard in months. Yeah, there's some issues between father and son. Ones that require hundreds of hours in family therapy sessions.

"You do realize I headed a few guys off at the pass so they wouldn't come in here and see Rory's feet mingled with yours, right?"

Eyes bugging out of my head, I plead with Devon to get Malcolm out of here. "Caught my nutsack in my zipper and Rory's helping me." Laughing silently, I'd piss my pants if it wasn't for the fact I just pissed a few minutes ago.

"Word of advice for next time." Malcolm's voice gets closer, like he's leaning against the stall wall. "If your zipper snags your sack again, I'd suggest you fix it at home. If you have roommates, maybe take it to Rory's loft, or the attic of the Spook House."

Okay, now I'm really going to piss my pants.

"Who are you to give such advice?" Devon turns back into a little puke around his dad. Dayum.

"Son." The sound of fabric sliding against the stall door signals that Malcolm isn't going anywhere until he's good and ready. "Sometimes Colin's sack gets stuck in his zipper, and I've got to help him out. But the difference is, I do it in under three minutes. If it's a difficult job– ya know, *really stuck in there* –I take it to the attic where we have as much time as we need. See, you've been in here for almost half an hour, and cops drink a lot of coffee… so they piss a lot too."

"Just go away, please." Dev goes from peeved to mortified. Stepping away from me, he scrubs at his face. "Advice duly noted and appreciated, now let us leave without an audience."

"Are you alright, son?" The concern in the father's voice has tears glistening in the son's eyes. "I'm not judging– just protecting you."

"Thanks, Dad," Devon's voice is soft, holding affection, like he's hugging his dad through the door. "I'll drop by after I visit the dealership."

"Okay, see you at home then." Footsteps tap across the tile floor, retreating. "Have a good evening, Rory."

"You too, Malcolm," I gulp out, words barely audible. As soon as the door shuts behind the man, I'm flipping out. "What exactly is a nutsack stuck in a zipper a euphemism for? And why is it happening to Colin? And why is your dad taking Colin to Auggie's attic? Three minutes?"

Chuckling sinisterly, Devon grabs hold of my t-shirt to pull me from the stall. Then tucks his hands into his trouser pockets. We exit the bathroom as if nothing happened, going down the hallway away from the large communal office area toward a long tunnel.

"Wait 'til we hit the parking lot– bunch of busybodies in the Batcave." In companionable silence, we traverse the tunnel at an incline. Light shines up ahead, then we're flowing out into the back parking lot filled with cop cars and personnel parking. "This is a fallout shelter, in case you're curious."

"I was actually." We head around the outside of the Courthouse, and I lead the way to my Challenger. "The Batcave's pretty neat."

"I like it– keeps life interesting." Devon and I pretend –or maybe it's not pretend –we're just two friends going car shopping. He slides into my passenger seat, running an appreciative hand over the dash. "Just guessing, but I'm assuming it's a euphemism for either handjobs or blowjobs. What else could be accomplished in under three minutes?"

"You're serious?" After checking traffic, I pull out and head in the direction of the Dodge dealership. "What now? Come again? Your dad? Colin?"

"You need to hang out with the Playroomers more," Devon teases me. "It's common knowledge that Dad messes around with Colin. Used to with Opal too, until my stepmom came into the picture."

"Clover?" I practically shout in outrage. "What?!"

"Fairport is not as stuffy as it seems," Devon mutters wryly. "Seriously, you're a member of the Playroom now. They're an entertaining lot to be around, even if you're just observing. Once a week, Auggie lets everyone back into the attic, with the other nights for specific members. Dad and Clover sneak in there with Colin on Saturday nights."

"I feel so–"

"Innocent," Devon supplies with a chuckle. "It was just massages with my dad– handsies, we all call it. But the rumor going around is that it's progressed to actual sex. Dad was only with my mom until Clover, and Clover was only with Sam. Why not live a little if it's not hurting anyone?"

"You have changed," I mutter in shock. "You were the most possessive asshole I'd ever met."

"In this, I have," Devon admits, no games or manipulations being played. He's just open, talking to me like one human being to another. "Bad shit happens, so I'm just going to accept people love me, in the only way they can. I don't get to dictate how they love me."

"You're mad at your dad…" I trail off, hoping Devon will fill in the blanks.

"You know how people blame others for their problems, because it's easier than taking responsibility for it?"

"Yeah," I mutter absentmindedly as I take an exit ramp.

"I love my dad, think he's an incredible human being who's flawed." Taking a deep breath, Devon expels it in a rush. "But he is to blame for what happened to me. I know it. He knows it. My doctors know it. It's not up for debate. So it's going to take a long time to work through it."

"Shit– that's heavy shit."

"Exactly." Devon reaches out, placing his palm on my thigh. After my instantaneous reaction to the touch, I realize it's not only Malcolm with a tactile fixation and skin hunger. "I'm sorry I cornered you in the bathroom, but I had a bad day and I needed to feel *something* for a few stolen moments, even if it was wrong."

"Why was your day bad?" My question is out of more than just curiosity. That protectiveness erupts again, where I want to make sure no one harms Devon, including himself.

"I'm an addict, Rory– I'll be an addict until the day I die." Sounding gutted, Devon has to pause to collect himself before he continues. "I got out of rehab on Sunday, and today's only Wednesday. All day, I kept thinking to myself how I can't possibly survive the next sixty or seventy *years* if four days nearly killed me."

Voice wavering, I'm terrified for Devon. "Do you want me to pull over?"

"No, I'm good." His fingers tighten on my thigh. It's not sexual. Anchoring. "I can't talk to people about this stuff, because I have to play sane and sober so I don't worry them to death. Dr. Delaney has a scale we use. One is no craving whatsoever, no need. Ten is where I end up using drugs."

Fingers threaded together until we're woven as one, I place our hands on the gearshift. "At the worst today, what was your number on the scale?" This is what Bethany was trying to drill in my head, saying we end up over-simplifying complex emotions.

It's not that I need Devon.

It's not that Devon needs me.

It's that we need each other for different yet complementary reasons.

"You're probably the only one I could admit this to," Devon whispers nearly inaudibly. "Nine-point-nine."

Releasing a shuddering breath of pure terror, I modulate my voice to appear calm and collected. "What kept you a tenth of a point away from using?"

"Ah– fuck." Dev laughs without humor, a sound so devoid of life I'm not sure I can handle it. "I'd love to say it was the thrill of buying a new car, but we both know that's a high that fades quickly."

Pulling into the dealership, my eyes light on all the beauties. But right now, I could give a shit less. "What then?" After throwing the Challenger into park, I turn to Devon.

"If I use, it's the same thing as committing suicide." Devon shifts his hand beneath mine, and I anticipate him pulling away. But he only gets a better grip. "I went months without touching anyone. It's different with Essie. I'm supposed to keep her safe, not the other way around."

Devon hedges my question, and it has my hair standing on end.

"Mixing my meds with street drugs will set off a toxic signal to my brain, like when you hear *'suicidal thoughts'* during a pharmaceutical commercial. Except that's not what will kill me. After rehab, that first hit usually is the lethal one."

"So black and white facts and fear stopped you?" Realizing how that sounded, I quickly backtrack. "I'm not calling you a coward for not using. You're the bravest person I've ever met because you fought it and didn't use."

"Knowing I'd feel safe for a few minutes today stopped me," Devon admits hesitantly. In case I couldn't read between the lines, he adds, "*You* make me feel safe."

"C'mon." Reaching for the door, I toss Devon a naughty look. It might not be healthy to run from your issues, but it's just as toxic to dwell in them. "Let's go have some fun."

"Oh." Eyes on the prize, Devon slips from my car, then weaves his way through the lot. "This one."

Chuckling a sound that is pure sex, I'm delighted someone finally gets it– the lure of a stunning lady. "Pitch Black is undeniably sexy on a Charger."

"It's brand-new, though." Voice dreamy, Devon's palms caress the body of the machine, coming to a stop at the door latch. "I should probably get something used." Reluctant to part with the car, he peers inside the window.

"You only live once," the salesman says from a few feet behind me. I felt Jake approach, so I didn't jump. "You don't choose a car– it chooses you."

"How am I supposed to say no between the two of you?" Devon grins up at Jake.

"You don't," we reply in unison, sharing a grin.

The guy graduated a year after Auggie. He's the son of the owner, but was never an asshole about it when we were in school.

I bought my first piece of shit from his dad, and the Challenger from Jake. I'm a lifelong customer who stops in a few times a month to drool over the new stock, pick up treats for my lady, and chat with Jake.

"How about a test-drive?" Jake coaxes, no doubt sensing Devon's reluctance.

"Jesus, if I drive it, I'll never give it back." With lust in his eyes, Devon smooths his palm over the mirror-shined hood.

"I've been coveting this car for weeks," I admit, knowing Jake's been stalking me slowly for the sale. "The fact that you made a beeline to it is telling."

"You're getting rid of your car?" Devon's disbelief is humorous. Eyes wide, mouth gaping open, he stares at me over his shoulder. "Why?"

"Oh, no." Chuckling, I feel guilty just thinking about cheating on my lady. "If I didn't think Beth would knee me in the nuts, she'd no longer be driving that pussy Toyota."

"Do you want me to sabotage it?" Jake offers, guffawing.

"Would you?" Hope underlies the amusement in my voice. "Seriously, I'm waiting for that tin can to kick it. Beth can pick out anything she wants–"

"As long as it's a Dodge," Jake banters with me as Devon looks on with a funny expression twisting his face– sort of jealous looking, actually. Do friends get jealous over their friends having different friends? They probably do.

"I'd need to finance it," Devon says after a heartbeat, and I have to bite my lip against a smirk. He is jealous, but of what, I have no idea. "I have no outstanding debt and a fulltime career with the county, a land-contract mortgage, and all of my bills are split four ways. Do you think I could swing it? And don't just say so to make a commission."

"We have a debt-to-living ratio sheet in my office." Jake reaches out to touch Devon, but lets his hand drop, no doubt hearing the gossip trickle through Fairport. "I may be a car salesman, but I'm not a smarmy asshole. I make sure my clients can afford the vehicle first, because I don't want to ruin their credit and have to take a car back."

"And you want them as a customer for life, and their children, and their friends and family," I tease Jake. Hand moving on its own accord, I cup the back of Devon's neck to soothe his anxiety. "You sure you don't want to test-drive it first?"

"Have you driven it?" Devon steps into me, causing my arm to rest on his shoulder. It looks like we're a couple, but I say the hell with it. Everyone in town knows Beth and Essie are our worlds, so I brush off the bizarre warmth radiating from my chest.

Chuckling that sexual note again, "A few times, actually," I admit, blushing.

"Then I don't need to." Devon takes me at my word, trusting me, and Jake looks back and forth between us, adding things together.

"C'mon into my office," Jake reels us in with the lure of a sexy machine, in the hopes of catching a hefty commission off the sale. "Oh, Rory– your lady's new floor mats came in this morning."

"They're going to look gorgeous," I purr, already mentally replacing them. Pulling Devon under my arm, I steer him toward the main building of the dealership. "You're okay with this, right? I'm not forcing you into something you don't want?"

"I want the Charger, Rory." Devon's walking forward with us, but his eyes are glued over his shoulder, in the direction of his new car. "One of the best memories from the academy was pit maneuvers."

"Just wait until you feel it hug corners at a high-rate of speed." Laughing, I pull Devon closer. "I probably shouldn't be telling you this, seeing as your profession is to arrest law-breakers like me. But I may have tested the handling of the beauty by going over a hundred on straight stretches and pushing it to the brink on the curves."

"Shut it." Jake snickers underneath his breath. "You're making me hard, and it's freaking my ass out."

"If I worked here," I mutter wryly. "I'd never go soft."

Devon's true laughter has Jake doing a double-take– that liquid sunshine mixed with dirty sex sound.

CHAPTER FIVE

"I didn't force you to buy the car, did I?" Second-guessing my actions, I fear my own lust caused Devon to buy the Charger I've been coveting. "You still have time to back out." Not in a real hurry to go home just yet, I take the scenic route via the back roads.

"I know better than anyone else how we only get one life," Devon mutters cryptically. "The responsible thing to do would've been to buy Essie a minivan and continue to have someone take me to work and drop me off."

"Responsible thing?" Barking a sharp laugh, "I'd rather walk than own a minivan."

"I can still hear what you were thinking last night." Devon refuses to look at me as he talks to the windshield. "It's one of the reasons today was so difficult. *Seventy years*, Rory. I kept thinking about how I'd never have any fun again. Always being in control. Always being responsible. Routines and schedules, with bland food and absolutely no stimulants. I gave up so much to be stable."

No sense in denying it, "I'm sorry I ever thought that."

"It was true." Devon turns, and his intense, dark stare burns into the side of my face. "It's either taking seventy years as I am, one day at a time, or not living to see tomorrow."

"Christ," I gulp out, getting overemotional.

"I'm getting the car I want, goddamn it... and I'm going to drive it fast, with the music I want to listen to blaring from the speakers, with the windows down, wind whipping me in the face... and I'm going to feel motherfucking alive for a few minutes a day."

"Good deal," I murmur sincerely, getting snared by the agony reflected in Devon's eyes. I have to blink in order to look away before we wreck. "Do you want me to pick you up from work tomorrow so you can go fetch it?"

"Ozzy's been driving the Pussy Magnet around. He picks me up from work after dropping off Clover's bag lunches to the guys."

I answer the question I'd asked earlier. Yes, a friend can get jealous of their friend having other friends. "Ozzy's a good kid." Voice gruff, I hadn't realized I was this needy. Which is probably why Beth's trying to get me out of her hair.

"I'm still me," Devon breaks into my thoughts. "I'm not being reasonable and accommodating by having Ozzy pick me up– I want to brag and show off. Maybe drag the boys along too."

"Oh!" Laughing, I pull off onto an old logging road. "Ozzy likes cars, does he?"

"Ren said the kid is always drooling with his head stuffed into motorcycle magazines, so I'm going to gloat tomorrow." Noticing where we are, Devon's confusion rings loudly. "Why are we stopping?"

Popping my door open, "You'll never hit nine-point-nine again on my watch." Hopping out, I reach into the back seat for a blanket. "Your place is crawling with people, and mine is gearing up for another night of drunkenness." Shutting the door, I expect Devon to follow me.

"Yeah, neither's good unless I want to hit ten," Devon mutters wryly, jerking my chain. "What are you going to do, Rory? Ravish me?" Raising a brow, he waits for my answer while helping me spread the blanket on the ground.

"I'd buy you a steak first," I volley back. "This is a trial and error type friendship, so hopefully this trial won't result in error."

"Huh?" Confusion looks good on the guy– he no longer appears to be three heartbeats away from slitting his own wrists with a jagged fingernail. The guy who taunted me in the bathroom earlier today makes a reappearance, and I want him to stay.

"Lie down on the ground."

"I *really* don't like to be told what to do," Devon reminds me, and it floods my mind with countless memories of our childhood.

"Do it anyway, boss," I tease, pointing at the blanket. "If we reach the error stage, just say the word *Red*."

"Somebody *did* sneak into the Playroom when it was at Rush, I see." With a wink, Devon flows fluidly to the ground like water. The prick is far too graceful for my sanity's sake.

"Maybe a little bit." Blushing like a bastard, I take a deep breath. "I'm going off a hunch here, so just say *Red* and it all stops."

"Got it." Lying on the ground, Devon wiggles around until he's comfortable. Dark hair framing his face, wicked eyes glowing up at me, I have to swallow down the rising lust, because now is not the time nor the place for it.

"You like hugging, the tighter the better." Kneeling next to Devon on the blanket, I haven't felt this nervous in a long time. It's a bit thrilling to experience for some reason.

"The first thing I did when I got home was force Ren to spoon me so I could sleep," Devon admits, eyelashes shuttering his gaze. "It did and didn't work. I feel like a paranoid bastard, not wanting my back to a room and having to face the door, how I'm not able to sleep alone anymore. But when it's Essie and me, I'm the one who has to protect her, comfort her– spoon her."

"I'm the one with the emasculating issues, so I get how you want to be the big, bad manly man and protect your woman, but sometimes you need it more."

"Yeah, but I'm not much bigger than Essie, so I've always been a target." Sighing, Devon covers his face with his forearm. "Since I was born, I only felt safe when I was in a small space devoid of people. Mom would snatch my wrist as I walked by, then go nuts on me. I could be walking by and get backhanded for no reason."

"This started before…" I trail off, refusing to voice what happened to Devon when he was fourteen. Reaching, I tug his forearm away from his face. Pausing, I wait until he looks at me. "You've never felt safe, have you?"

"No," is said in a quiet voice with the impact of a gunshot. "Not for one second. As the oldest, it was my job to take care of my siblings *and* Mom. It's why Dad and I have a lot of road to cover. Dad was supposed to protect me from everyone– from

Mom, from the nightmare, and from myself. So I can't stand for him to hug me anymore."

"Remember– *Red*." All Devon craves is for someone he trusts to have his back. But during a hug, it's still exposed. Panting breathlessly, terrified Devon will flip out on me, I cover his entire body with mine, pressing his back into the protective earth. "Let me know if I'm squishing you with my mammoth ass."

Expression already looking drugged, Devon melts onto the ground. The more of my weight I press into him, the more he turns to a puddle of goo. "Yeah... *this*." Another question is answered for me– having Devon Mason writhing beneath me is a transcendental experience.

I don't even bother hiding how goddamn hard I am. Pressing my erection into his hip, Devon shocks me by sliding his leg to the side. "Shit!" I hiss, body on fire from the contact of his bulge with mine.

"I didn't say red," Devon whispers against the side of my throat, hands landing on my ass. "Stop trying to pull away when I make you hard– been doing it since forever."

"You disturb me," I mutter in a grumpy tone, eyes rolling back into my head because the bastard is manipulating my ass with his fingertips.

Laughing that intoxicating laugh, Devon's body vibrates beneath mine. "*This* is fun. Don't you want to fuck Beth anymore?"

"What?" I jerk a few inches away so I can glare down at him. "So they have been talking behind my back."

"No, actually." Devon grins up at me evilly. "Let's just say Robin was offering me some sadistic hugging in the attic on Monday, and he let it slip there was a guy in need of my friendship. Rob didn't say your name, but it wasn't difficult to deduce when he brought up how our women wouldn't mind. He said it wasn't about sex, but I'd want it to be."

"So Beth hasn't been talking about me?" Not trusting what I'm hearing, I narrow my eyes.

"Nah, not about whatever this is." Devon looks innocent, but that means jackshit when it comes to this guy. "I'm sure Essie knows, but I'm not going to ask her when I can just ask you myself."

"You and Beth had a one-on-one conversation Monday night…" I trail off, asking but not asking.

"*About me*," Devon stresses. "Not you, okay?"

"Okay."

"Relax," he coaxes, drawing me back down to cuddle on top of him. "I was joking about you not wanting Bethany. Hell, I caught you drooling over Essie's tits. So what's freaking you out so much? Every time I show you I'm horny too, you pull away from me."

"Don't you feel guilty?"

"No, I don't." Devon's hands reach up to cup my shoulders. "I almost died," he whispers with tears in his eyes. "I can't help how I feel or what I want, and it doesn't change how devoted to Essie I am."

"But we're–"

"I can count the amount of people I've been attracted to on one hand, and I've had even less consensual sex." Eyes slipping shut, Devon pours it out. "This isn't about sex, but it is– it's all tied up together. But, no, I don't feel guilty. We're just holding each other, because it feels good, not because we're fucking around on the girls."

"But we are hard, and it will lead to sex." Glaring down at Devon, I can't fathom why this isn't making him feel guilty. "I'm not delusional, I know when someone is seducing me."

Releasing a sadistic laugh, Devon's looking a bit high. "This is fun. This is exactly what I need. This isn't the end of the world. This isn't life or death. I'm not fucking you today, so calm yourself."

Lifting up on my arms, I scoff. "Making assumptions, aren't you?"

"No, I don't think I am," Devon mutters without a lick of arrogance. "So what's your malfunction? You still want Bethany, anyone can see that. So why is Robin worried about you?"

"I may or may not have had a meltdown when Isis, Auggie, and Rob invaded my apartment to tell me they're pregnant."

"Ah– that would be why I lived at the Spook House for less than twelve hours and moved into my house a few weeks early. The girls refused to deal with that bullshit… so what happened?"

Laughing without humor, I crawl to straddle Devon's thighs. "Let's just say I told the deviant trio I was sick of being their shadow and living their life." Turning away, I mumble inaudibly out the side of my mouth, "And I told them I was bisexual."

"No shit, Sherlock." Devon's taunting laughter has me punching him in the chest. Catching my fist in his palm, he sobers. "I've known that since puberty."

"Are you straight?"

"I don't know." Eyebrows knitting in the center of his forehead, Devon truly thinks over my question. "I really don't know. Sex for me is complicated– it's never been easy. If you asked me that when I was fourteen, I would've said straight because I was obsessed with Essie. I would've probably still said straight three months ago. Today, the jury's out, and I don't care. I want what I want when I want it, consequences be damned because I'm choosing to live."

"If someone asks you, how will you respond?"

"If it's one of my therapists or doctors, I'll tell them the truth." Devon reaches out to smooth his palms down my chest, fingers biting in lightly. "If the girls or you asked, I'd do the same. But if anyone else does, I'll say straight. Not because it's acceptable, but because it's a less complicated answer."

"If someone asks me, what should I say?"

"Tell 'em the truth." Fingers curl into my belt loops, tugging and releasing me until I'm rocking slightly. "Tell 'em you're bi, because you are. It's not up for debate. You've always known it."

"I don't know if I always have," I mutter, feeling insecure and indecisive.

"People get so hung up on this bullshit– I don't get it. Ren's a total homophobe, but he's messed up in the head. We're just people, so why does it matter who we fuck? Weston's gay, but he's just Weston to me. If he wasn't gay, it'd be fucking bizarre. You're Rory, and I've never thought twice about you liking both girls and guys. You were the guy who stopped being my friend because I gave you wood during a hug."

"Ass." Punch landing with a hollow thud, I leave my hand where it rests against Devon's chest. "I'm still floored over your transformation from possessive psycho to enlightenment."

"That's a conversation best left for another day and another place." Devon's lips curl into a wicked smirk, showing he has one helluva secret. "I'll tell you tomorrow."

"Stringing me along so you're guaranteed I'll hang out with you another day?" Too late, I realize I'm flirting with Devon. But I don't care because it feels damn good doing it.

"Maybe." Devon's smirk brightens, like he can read my mind. "Crazy Devon is entertaining, and you know it. You never know how I'm going to behave in any given situation, lending a dangerous air to all of our interactions."

"You are creepy as fuck." Grinning down at him, I realize I'm rocking my hips back and forth, rubbing up against his thighs.

"Just for future reference, my favorite type of hug is you lying on top of me."

"Shit!" Shuddering, my eyes slip shut, but a phone trilling cuts off whatever else I had to say.

"And the digital leash tightens," Devon growls, not making a move to retrieve his phone.

Vibrating near my knee, my hands seek the blasted thing. Palm skating over Devon's hip, he arches slightly so I can reach inside his front pocket. On the exit, my knuckles rasp against his bulge, and he presses closer.

Rolling his eyes, Devon hits the icon for speaker phone. "Yes, Ren– I'm still very much alive and sober."

Just like with his dad, Devon's personality shifts to bitter as he speaks to his brother. I watch the struggle hidden in the depths of his eyes, as he tries to forget the past and forgive.

"We're eating at Dad and Clover's tonight," echoes slightly from the device as it rests on Devon's chest.

Moving to pull away, Devon stops me by grabbing for my hand. Twining our fingers together, he rubs our hands over his lean torso, dipping beneath his shirt.

"What time?" Devon mutters absentmindedly while showing me how he wants to be touched. Skin warm and smooth, wiry hairs tickle my knuckles.

"*Seven,*" Ren sounds hurried. "*You're gonna be late. Where the hell are you, bro?*"

I stopped paying attention to everything around me the instant Devon began rubbing his own cock with my hand. Hard, the perfect handful, I wish there wasn't a pair of trousers between our flesh.

"*You better not be alone.*" Ren's worry is like a bucket of ice being poured over my junk. It has the same effect on Devon, cock deflating in an instant. "*Why are you panting?*"

Coming to the rescue, which is why Bethany set us up in the first place, I defend Devon to his over-protective, smothering brother. "Hey, Ren. Devon and I just got done car shopping, and we stopped to get some fresh air on one of the old logging roads."

"*Oh, wow… Hey, Rory.*"

"I'll have Devon home in about fifteen minutes."

"*Okay, good. Dad will be relieved.*" But it sounds more like Ren's the one who's relieved. "*I'll see ya at home, bro– love you.*"

"Love you too." Even with his words clipped with bitterness, anyone could hear the obvious affection Devon holds for his brother. Jabbing a finger on the screen, Devon flashes me a *do you see what I'm dealing with* look.

"Are you ever alone?" Curiosity gets the better of me as I stumble to my feet.

"No," Devon answers without hesitation, flowing to his feet with the agility of a cat. "It's been almost three months since I've been truly alone. At the center, we were monitored continuously, with only the perception of privacy. Since I got home, I have actual privacy in the bathroom, but I can feel everyone in the house terrified I'm harming myself in there."

"Jesus Christ." I pitch the blanket into the back seat, then slide into the driver's seat. "How are you going to deal with that?"

Devon sits next to me, passenger side door shutting with a hollow thud. "Why do you think I've been seducing you into being my friend?" The words are taunting, but the tone is serious. "No more autonomy. I can't be alone– I know this. I understand why, and I can empathize with their terror. But I can't be around them right now."

"So you picked me," I murmur softly, unsure how I feel about that, as I back out of the logging road.

"Sunday," Devon begins hesitantly. "When you showed up to help us move, I liked how you felt. I liked how I felt being near you, so that's why. I wanted to hang out with you. I can be me without putting on a sane and sober and everything is fucking hunky-dory act. You didn't go postal and cry when I said I hit nine-point-nine today."

"Fair enough," I grunt gruffly, but secretly I'm radiating warmth from the inside out over what Devon just admitted.

The rest of the ride is taken in silence, but it's a healthy kind of quiet, where we're both thinking and not feeling alone in our thoughts. Going on a hunch, I pull up outside of the Pink Taco Hut instead of the Shithole, figuring that's where Devon was supposed to be.

"Thanks for the ride." Devon turns to reach for the door, then looks at me over his shoulder. "I can't fucking wait to drive the Charger." As the door opens, my heart beats out of my chest.

"Wait!" Grabbing forcefully, I twist my fingers into Devon's shirt, even though I know it's a bad idea with his issues. "Promise me something," I demand.

Surprisingly, Devon's not fazed by my abrupt movements and near violent touch. "I'm too paranoid and cautious to agree to an open-ended agreement, no matter who it's with."

"Just…" I smooth the wrinkles out of Devon's shirt. "Just promise me you'll call if you ever reach a seven, okay? No matter what time of day or place, you'll call me."

"I promise," Devon vows, truly meaning it. "Do you want to know what the lowest number I've had since I entered rehab was?"

"Yeah, I do." Knowing there are eyes on us, I don't dare pull Devon into a hug goodbye, so I settle on patting his chest instead.

"Four," Devon admits reluctantly, getting choked up. "Even when my brother was holding me, every thought was purely panic-driven."

"You amaze me," I whisper, but I'm unsure if Devon hears me or not.

"Nine-point-nine was the highest I reached today." Devon slides out of the seat to stand on the sidewalk, then he leans back into the car. "But for a little while, I was riding steady at a one."

Gasping with tears burning my eyes, I can't speak, let alone breathe.

Lips curling into a smile I haven't seen since we were kids, Devon leans back out of the car. "The next seventy years are going to be a cakewalk."

I'm still idling at the curb, long after the door closes, hearing Devon's *thank you* echoing in my ears.

CHAPTER SIX

"What's on your agenda for the rest of today?" Beth's giving me her undivided attention before she's off to school. Every day we share at least one meal together, which happens to be lunch today.

Those are the rules: at least one meal together, and we have to sleep in the same bed, side-by-side, all night long, every single night, waking up together in the morning. Most days, we cram in a few episodes of Beth's favorite shows and a walk around town. Once a week or so, we turn into little kids and decorate Rush's parking lot with sidewalk chalk. Mysteriously, Robin always pops in to help, with Auggie's supervision. They swear they can hear the art calling them from across town. I say they're nosy bastards with amazing talent.

Fairport's denizens are now calling our parking lot a tourist attraction.

"Now that Isis has backed off," I murmur, feeling like a shitheel. "I have a lot more time on my hands."

"It was for the best," Beth reminds me. "Those three are like parasites. If you give them an inch, they take a light-year."

"You love 'em, admit it," I tease. "Auggie's living next door again. Didn't know if you noticed since he sneaks in and out."

"Yeah, I was surprised he didn't hide out in the loft above Revamped." Bethany jiggles the two-liter Coke bottle in my line of sight, asking if I want more. Before I'm halfway through shaking my head a single time, she's emptying it into her glass. "None of us can step in this time, Rory."

Beth's using her '*I mean it*' voice, and I can't help but smile at the ridiculousness. She honestly believes I'm going to get in the middle of their bullshit again, when I finally feel free of their pull.

"There's a child involved now, so they have to get over themselves and make it work." Borderline angry, Beth stabs her fork into a slice of cucumber like she's murdering it. My wife rarely shows negative emotions, so I know it's bad.

Getting a clue, "Which one of them is pestering you instead of me?" It's been quiet on my end, except for a cryptic text from Robin this morning, requesting my presence at the Spook House tonight.

"All of them." The look of horror etched across Bethany's face has me getting up from my side of the table to crouch next to her. "Rob's being... good, actually. But Isis is filled with rage and Auggie's a ball of confusion."

"I'm so fucking sorry." Rubbing Beth's thigh, I try to take that look off her face. "I'll take my friends back."

"No!" She grabs my hand, hugging it to her chest. "No, don't. We're good. You're good. You need to be happy."

"You're not happy," I point out, using the arm she's hugging like a lifeline to draw her from her chair to the sofa. "All I do all day is random clerical work for Rush, then manage the club at night. It's easy as fuck. Your education matters. I'll deal with my fucked up friends myself."

"I'm not unhappy," Beth stresses, pleading with me with her eyes. "I look at this as practice. I'm the one studying to help people fix their lives. This is about as hands-on as anyone could get."

"You need to have a life too, little pup." Dragging Beth into my lap, I cuddle her up against my chest. "You need to have fun, de-stress, get away from it all for a few minutes."

"Babe, I do that." Grabbing my face in her tiny hands, Bethany peers into my eyes. "I love my life– I do exactly as I want. This week alone, I spent a lot of time at the salon, which was basically Essie and me primping each other and gossiping. We went dress shopping, hit a few party supply stores, and we took my mom out to lunch. In the middle of a study group last night, we did shots and played Presidents and Assholes to relax. After my afternoon class, we're having another study group, and I'm bringing a bottle of tequila from the stock room. Then we'll study for a few more hours to sober up before the drive home."

"The summer session sounds a lot more lax than I expected it to be," I mutter wryly, getting a kick out of Bethany acting her age for once.

"Graduate program actually." Beth blushes a pretty shade of pink, eyes darting away from mine. "We've had four or five years of practice, and we're all old enough to drink."

"One of these nights, you should cut out the middleman and study here at Rush– on the house." Then I think the better of it. "Unless this is your *me* time and you don't want me getting involved."

Lips quirking up sweetly, Bethany gazes at me as if I'm her favorite person in the whole wide world. "Babe, that's the best fucking thing I've heard all week. I'll set something up for next week." Kisses are planted on the tip of my nose, my eyelids, and then my lips. "I love spending time with you. I'm not trying to pawn you off on Devon– I honestly believe you two will click."

"This way you don't have to worry about me when you're busy." Growling underneath my breath, I relive the guilt I spewed to my wife last night at two a.m. after closing. It was a cry in my beer moment while Beth sat across the booth silently laughing at me.

"You're walking a little funny today," I whisper against her cheek while running the tip of my nose along her eyebrow. My wife got hotter than I was, and she only heard about me rubbing Devon's dick through his pants. Details– I gave 'em to her, and more. "Hmm... why is that, little pup? Is your pussy sore?"

"That was *intense*," Beth releases breathlessly, shuddering in my arms. "I didn't think I'd live to see the day you'd eat me out... on a motherfucking tabletop..." Gasping for air, my wife is wiggling shamelessly in my lap, trying to get some relief by grinding on my swollen dick. "In a booth... in the middle of Rush."

"Here I thought it was fucking you on the bar that had you going wild." Getting a little too turned on, I have to grip my junk and squeeze.

"We have to do a repeat," Beth pants into my ear, all the while she's rubbing her thighs together. "Soon."

"That can be arranged." Lips trailing along Beth's neck, my fingers slip between her thighs. "NO!" I groan in frustration as two cellphones go off simultaneously. Beth's is ringing and mine is the text alert. "I only needed thirty seconds 'til liftoff."

Smirking smugly as she climbs off my lap, Beth gives my package a rough squeeze. "Well, maybe I need a lot more time than that." She snags her cell off the table. "And I'm too sore right now... Hey, Ma. What's up?"

Sighing, I go about my husbandly duties. As I clean up our lunch, I pretend I'm not listening in on their conversation. "Yeah, I'm not leaving for school until two. I can stop over and help you hook up your new DVR real quick."

Now that Beth's preoccupied, I drain all the Coke in her glass. Chuckling evilly, I almost choke on a burp.

"See ya in a few... Yeah, love you too, Ma." Beth sets her sights on me as she presses end on the call. "Now, where were we?"

Puckered lips head my way, but I have to get a question answered first. "Do you think I'm needy?"

"What?" Beth snorts loudly, finding me utterly ridiculous. "I think you're caring, giving, and kind. I think you're hotter than Hades, and you make my pussy weep. I think you have a lot to offer this world, and people take advantage of it. I'm in a place right now, where I'm the only one who can accomplish my goals, and it's hurting your masculinity because you *can't* help me."

"In walks Devon–"

"Rory." Beth sighs in exasperation, grabbing for the dishtowel in my hand. "Essie cut my hair the other day, and highlighted it. I'm sore, because she waxed my pussy lips and bleached my asshole this morning." Beth waits a heartbeat to stare at my gape-mouthed expression.

"I did those things for you, by the way... Do you know what we talked about? *You.* We talked about how your big dick felt incredible inside me, and how fucking sweet you were to wake me up with a fresh cup of coffee. We felt relieved that Devon only woke to one nightmare last night. We talked about how Essie's pelvis hurts because she's pregnant and how her nipples are leaking already."

"I don't get where you're going with this, Bethany," I stammer, blushing with mortification. "I really don't."

"In my study group, we're discussing serial rapists who target women who look like their mothers... I held Isis's hand yesterday morning while we visited the clinic to confirm her pregnancy, and then I talked Auggie down from a panic attack."

"I can't help you with these things," I murmur, realization hitting.

"Your budding bromance with Devon has nothing to do with you being bisexual, Rory. I need to be needed, and you need to be needed, but we're entirely self-sufficient with lives separate from each other. This is why I feared getting married, remember? But we agreed we're equals who come together– we can't be codependents. Do you know who you can help? Do you know who you want to help?"

"Devon," I say with absolute certainty. "We were put on this earth to help people who need us, because we were blessed to not need–"

"But when one of us does need help, we have each other." Beth's arms slide around my hips, drawing our bodies together. "Babe, you're not clingy or needy– you're amazing. You deserve to be happy, to have anything you want, and I love you too much to take it away from you. On the flip side, I expect you to love me enough to give me the space, to not only grow, but to flourish too."

"I'm finally getting it." Relaxing, breathing deeply for the first time in nearly a week, I finally get it– finally get what Beth's been trying to tell me since she began avoiding me all those months ago. She was worried I was going to put her in a tiny box as a wife and mother who lived *my* life. She's not pushing me away right now. She doesn't want to live my life, and she doesn't want me to live hers. She wants me to have a full life of my own, walking beside her the entire journey.

Worried because I didn't voice any of that out loud, and that's something I always try to do, Bethany's expression warps into fear. "You don't feel like I'm rejecting you, do you?"

"No." I squeeze Beth to my chest. "I'm not gonna lie. At first, I was jealous of your friendship with Essie, but happy for you too. I've been struggling, feeling rejected, and pushed at Devon. But I think I'm starting to get it."

"Get what?" Beth uses her cerebral powers to make sure I understand what I'm feeling. She sometimes makes me repeat things on purpose. The girl is going to annihilate her future clients.

"I'm never going to cut your hair, because I'll ruin it. You can't gossip about me to me, because I'm *me*. I'm not gonna wax your pussy or bleach your butthole– *you seriously do that? –* because I'll be terrified to hurt you."

Smirking at my butthole comment, Beth turns saucy. "And I can humor you 'til the cows come home, but I could give a shit less about cars. I listen, and I respond, but it pretty much goes right over my freakin' head."

"And when you rant about contouring YouTube tutorials, I think you're insane, because everyone ends up looking like a breathing mannequin in the end."

"My God, I love you." Beth cups my face in her palms, drawing my lips down to hers. Words are interspersed with puckered smooches. "So fucking much. You know that, right?"

"Prove it– stop forcing me to watch late nineties teenage soap operas." Beth's newest obsession is Dawson's Creek, and now she's threatening to move onto the twenty-first century with One Tree Hill and The OC. "Watch those with Essie. Hell, recruit Willow and her sisters too, but leave me out of it. Let's find something to watch together. *Recent* shows."

"Deal, but no more Vin Diesel or The Rock." Bethany rolls her eyes, never understanding the power The Fast and the Furious has over me. "Dwayne Johnson is *not* hot." She always smirks when I turn into a blubbering mess while watching Paul Walker.

"Oh, you've done it now." I pick Beth up, tossing her over my shoulder. "Don't be insulting my hero." I grab her purse on my way by the table, making sure her cellphone is still clutched in her palm. "Time to go visit your momma."

Reaching for the door, Beth shrieks, "Wait! I need my books and laptop."

Depositing the little minx in the hallway, making sure her feet are firmly rooted on the floor first, I run back into our apartment to grab her insanely heavy bag filled with school junk. Racing back, panting, "You're going to be late for class– you know damned well your mom isn't going to let you leave easily."

"Remind me again why I thought going year-round was a good idea?" Shouldering her bag, Bethany's body goes lopsided from the added weight on her left side.

"You called me a slacker when I tried to stop you from signing up for the summer session, remember?" After stealing a kiss, I push at her shoulders with my palms. "Off you go, smarty pants. Go conquer the world."

"Two a.m.?" Whoever says an eyebrow arching can't be sexy and suggestive is delusional.

"Booth or bar, your pick." Swooping in, I steal another kiss, adding tongue for good measure. "I've got to see what that bleaching nonsense is all about."

"Later, player..." Bethany sings, skipping down the steps to the main floor.

Walking on air, I breeze back into the apartment, whistling while I finish picking up our lunch mess. My cellphone blinking reminds me of the text alert I received a while ago.

Devon Mason: *Up for some fun?*

—Shit yeah. When & where?

Devon Mason: *Parking lot portal to the Batcave. 1:45*

—You better bring the fun, bub.

Devon Mason: *Just wait & see.*

Ending our conversation with a devil emoji seemed more than appropriate. Rushing to get everything put where it goes, I have just enough time to take a leak– not going there again with Devon in a public restroom.

CHAPTER SEVEN

Heart beating out of my chest, I take up a lackadaisical pose against the wall on the backside of the Courthouse. Devon's idea of fun is terrifying, so why do I feel so exhilarated right now?

Arriving a few minutes early, I've calmed myself by chatting with the friendly faces of Fairport's Police Department as they come and go into the tunnel leading to the depths of the Batcave. I made Nina's day by telling her she looked gorgeous, then gave her a big hug and a kiss on the cheek. She made mine by squeezing my bicep and teasing me with a Little Red Riding Hood, "*My. My. My. What big arms you have,*" before disappearing to field 911 calls.

Everyone makes noise when they walk. The fact that I don't hear anything, yet feel light and air displacing from the tunnel, tells me my companion for the afternoon is arriving. Devon is the most agile, sure and light-footed creature on the planet.

"So," I break away from the wall at the exact moment Devon steps from the tunnel. "Thoughts on The Fast and the Furious franchise."

Spooked that I sensed him when everyone thinks him a Ninja, Devon does a double-take. "Anyone who really knows Bethany, knows she's obsessed with collecting DVDs–"

"And she hates action movies and shows," I add in, following Devon through the parking lot to the shittiest, oldest police car.

"I see a Saturday spent in front of a TV in our near future." Devon flashes me an evil grin as he slides into the driver's seat. "Hop in."

"So you like action movies?" After a lifetime of being a good boy, sitting in a cop car feels strange, because that usually signals you did something bad, unless you're a cop like Devon.

"Just blame my meds when I cry through the earlier movies with Paul Walker." Not bothering to look around for other cars, Devon pulls out of the parking lot like he owns the road. Our fellow drivers get out of the way. Those who slow down–terrified they'll get a speeding ticket for going the speed-limit – Devon snarls at them as he passes on both the left and right.

"You're disturbing," I mutter my new standard response when Devon freaks my ass out.

"Seriously!" Devon gestures to the cars in front of us. "Go the goddamn speed limit. I'ma arrest their asses for disrupting the flow of traffic by driving like little old ladies. They're fucking up the timing on the red lights."

"You're not going to drive the Charger like this, are you?" Devon's dark gaze connects with mine, for far too long, and I fear we'll wreck. "That's machine abuse, and I'll have to take custody of your new car."

"It's the car and the badge, you know?" Devon finally looks back at the road. "It's like a protective bubble is surrounding this car, because Fairport has skittish, law-abiding denizens. When I'm driving a personal vehicle, I follow all traffic laws."

"Except speed limits?" I wager a guess, grinning like a villain because I sure as fuck don't mind the posted speeds. Nothing's as exhilarating as opening up the Challenger as far as she'll go, the purr of her engine vibrating my foot.

"They're merely a suggestion when no one's looking, ya know?" Devon's foot presses down on the accelerator, going at least twenty miles-per-hour faster than he should, about the speed I go. Face glowing with life, "Just don't get caught."

"Or wreck."

"Or wreck," Devon agrees, sobering. Abruptly turning into a hidden driveway, taking the curve at a rate of speed that has goosebumps beading on my flesh, we come to a jarring stop. "Or get caught."

Window down, radar gun in hand, Devon jabs a USB stick into a port in the dashboard with the other. Music floods the car, bass pounding. Not satisfied with the volume, Devon's cranking it up until it's nearly impossible to speak.

Free.

Devon looks free.

Devon looks free, happy, and alive.

He's got to be riding a one right now.

Some cars Devon clocks, others he doesn't even bother. The slow drivers piss him off more than the ones driving a few miles over the speed-limit. None of them seem to interest him.

Super-sonic hearing, Devon's hand flashes out to turn the techno beating song down to a low hum. Then he's pressing a button on the mic clipped to his collar, radio coming to life, when I never heard it.

"*Vibrates slightly*," Devon mouths to me out the side of his mouth. "Chief Mason finally sleeps naked, but he still reads Historical Romance novels. Only this time he's sharing them with his new wife."

"*Devon, goddammit. Where are you?*" Malcolm sounds furious, yet there's a note of humor, or maybe relief, like this is something the father and son did in the past.

"I'm suddenly experiencing déjà vu, sir." Devon's response makes my assumption correct.

"*Are you driving Kyle's car?*"

"Why ever would you think that, Dad?" Devon smirks at me, devious expression belying his calm tone of voice.

"*Devon,*" Malcolm snarls. "*Kyle told you to hang for a minute while he fetched a coffee. He just jogged in here saying both you and his car are missing.*"

"Wow, Dad. What kind of police station are you running? Kyle must be a shitty cop to misplace both a human being and a thousand-pound automobile."

Devon asked if I was up for some fun. A guy who's on mood stabilizers would find jacking a police cruiser fun. Jesus Christ!

"*Wait, what is that I hear?*" Malcolm pauses. "*Is your shit-tastic techno stick shoved in the port to the mobile laptop again?*"

"Déjà vu, Dad– serious case of déjà vu." Devon busts out laughing, his real laugh from when we were kids, mixed with an adult sound that can only be described as sinful. "Do I hear you chuckling in the background, Chief Mason?"

"*Dry cough.*" Malcolm clears his throat a few times, but a few chuckles escape, and we can hear a mixture of different reactions in the background from Devon's coworkers. "*Allergies.*"

"Damn those seasonal allergies. The pollen count is wicked high today, isn't it, Dad?"

"Why are you in Kyle's car? You know you're on restricted duty for the next year."

"I'm doing a ride-along, sir," Devon replies without missing a beat, thoroughly enjoying the banter he's sharing with his dad.

"You are well aware I have a visual on Oliver right now, Devon."

"Tell Ozzy I said hi– another concerned citizen is doing a ride-along, sir."

"Your imaginary friends don't count, son," Malcolm banters back, and I have to bite my bottom lip to stop a childish giggle from erupting. *"Oliver is the only civilian who is approved for ride-alongs."*

Tone serious, dark eyes toying with me, "We're having another nutsack stuck in the zipper emergency, sir."

"We must be using that euphemism for different things, son."

"Sarcasm goes right over your head, doesn't it, Dad?"

"Devon!"

"Yes, sir?"

"Get that car back here ASAP."

"As soon as my ride-along companion and I are finished with the summer school speeders."

"Lord, save us from your obsession with naughty high schoolers."

"Just doing my civic duty, sir." As if by magic, traffic picks up as school lets out for the day.

"Fine, I give up." Malcolm's sigh of frustration echoes in the car. *"At least tell me who's with you... and they better be a living, breathing human being, not someone you made up out of thin air."*

"Fairport's best club manager, sir."

"Jesus, maybe we do mean the same thing when it comes to that euphemism."

"I'm guessing we do, Dad." Mouth gaping open, I'm floored Devon just admitted that. "But right now we're actually sitting at my favorite speed-trap. I needed..." Devon's voice turns soft, quiet– raw. Real. "I needed to be able to breathe, Dad. I know

I'm not allowed to be alone, so let me pick who's babysitting me, okay?"

"Rory?" Malcolm calls, testing, because high and crazy, or sane and sober, Devon is the most manipulative person on the planet. A skilled liar. *"How's my son actually doing?"*

Devon holds the mic close to my face, so Malcolm can hear my response. "Good, actually." I reach over to curl my hand around Devon's firm thigh. "He's enjoying himself, just having a little fun, with someone who lets him be himself."

"Okay." Malcolm audibly swallows, as if it's physically killing him not to be in control of the situation. *"Son, just be back to the station by three-thirty."*

"Will do, Dad," sounds a helluva lot like an *I love you.* "See ya then." Devon flashes me his patented *see what I'm dealing with here* look. His finger flicks off his mic, cutting off all communication with the station. "I know I fucked up, and I deserve the consequences. I accept it, but sometimes I just need to breathe."

"I get it– believe me, I do."

Music volume raised to brain-bleeding levels, I watch Devon click the radar gun on passing high schoolers thrilled to be out of summer school for the week. Devon chuckles sadistically as they fly by, but so far he hasn't driven out of his hidey hole for anyone, even the douche going fifteen miles-per-hour too fast.

"Whoa…" Leaning forward, I barely get time to brace myself on the dash as Devon cranks the wheel, tosses the radar gun, and takes off like a bat out of hell. "Holy shit! How fast was he going?"

Car driving over ruts, I'm tossed all over the front seat, banging my hip into things most cars don't contain. I have to yell over the volume of the music, knowing better than to turn it down.

Grinning like a high idiot, Devon peels out onto the road, chasing the kid down with lights swirling and siren blazing. "Eighty-three in a fifty-five… my kinda kid."

"What?!" I shout, confused as to why Devon respects the humungous size of the kid's balls.

"Time to put the fear of God into him, so he doesn't kill himself or anybody else. You need to learn how to handle a car before you drive at those speeds." Devon whips in behind where the kid is parked along the side of the road. "Dammit, I thought he'd give me a longer chase."

Turned to the side, Devon gazes at me, and it's like a light switch being flipped, how quickly he goes from glowing with an adrenaline rush to the seriousness of a police officer doing his civic duty. No matter what, there's always a chance of danger— the possibility a cop's walking into a situation he will be carried out of in a body bag. With Devon, the danger is part of the appeal of the job.

After turning off his music, Devon hits his mic, then spews a bunch of numbers and letters and codes I don't understand, checking the driver for warrants, and he gets the all-clear from Nina at dispatch.

"Showtime." Devon grins at me, then schools his expression before exiting the vehicle.

In awe, I watch as Devon swaggers up to the ancient, tan sedan, utility belt swaying on his hips. He's small for his gender and age, the smallest person in his entire family, including Raven. But no one could deny the commanding power radiating from the man— confidence, not arrogance.

Devon must recognize the occupants, because he's flipping his notebook open instead of going for a weapon. With a rasp of his knuckles, he's exuding charm as the window rolls down.

Laughing, joking around with the kids, Devon spends a good ten minutes giving a lecture with a wide smile on his face. It's obvious his job gives immense meaning to his life. Stepping back, he gives a salute and a wave, waiting for the car to pull out before walking back to me.

"Let Josh off with a warning," Devon mutters breathlessly as he slides into the driver's seat. "Good kid."

"What the actual fuck?" spills from my shocked lips.

"I know every kid in this town, and not just because it's my job. Josh's family is dirt poor. He's in summer school because he had a fulltime job last school year and couldn't keep up with his homework."

"Yeah, but... eighty-three in a fifty-five. He could kill himself."

Devon pulls out onto the road, driving cautiously, bypassing the hidey hole we exited earlier, headed back into town. "Once I pull someone over, everyone knows I'm there, so they all drive exactly fifty-five. Small window of opportunity to teach lessons."

"Again, eighty-three in a fifty-five," I repeat, confused like a sonofabitch.

"Ya know, Jake Haines of Haines Dodge?" Devon reminds me, as if we didn't just see Jake yesterday. "Steve– Jake's little brother –is a total asshole. He was in the passenger seat, egging Josh on, I just know it. So I warned them how I'll be on the lookout, and the next time, I'll give Steve a fine, no matter if he's the passenger or not. I *loathe* entitled fucktwats."

Staring at the side of Devon's face, I realize he has a ginormous heart for such a sadistic bastard. "Let me guess... if you gave Josh a fine, he'd probably have to sell that piece of shit car to pay for it, have points on his license, and would have to quit summer school to work more."

"Yeah, and it's Steve's fault." Devon pulls into the parking lot at the Courthouse. "I know assholes like him. He'll get good kids into trouble, never have any consequences himself, and live like this for life, ruining his friends' lives. *Those* are the people I arrest."

"Things that appear simple are actually complex," I channel Bethany.

"Exactly." Devon pulls the keys from the ignition. "Time to face the music."

Shutting the door behind me, I follow Devon across the parking lot. "You gonna be okay?"

"Yeah," Devon murmurs softly, lashes lowering in what I'd call coyness if he was female. "Dad will lecture me, but only because he's terrified. I'll let him hug me, pretending my skin isn't trying to crawl off my bones from the anxiety of it all. Then Ozzy and I will load the Pussy Magnet up with kids to go pick up the Charger."

"You're gonna rat Steve out to his big brother, aren't you?" Jake will be peeved, because he's a good guy.

"Nope." Devon's eyes twinkle mischievously. "I'm going to tell his daddy. The kid's fifteen, been bragging about how Daddy's giving him a brand-new Dodge for his birthday."

"Jesus," I hiss, rubbing a palm over my scalp. "That kid will be getting a tricycle now, won't he?"

"Did I bring the fun, or what?" Devon waves goodbye, then enters the tunnel to the Batcave. Before I can reply, "That was only the beginning, Rory– only the beginning," echoes back at me.

CHAPTER EIGHT

"Why exactly did you drag me up here?" Leveling a potent look at Robin, I sit down on the antique sofa, suspicion roiling in my guts. "I'm going to be late for work too."

"It's a Thursday." Robin rolls his eyes, sitting across from me on a ginormous throne that swallows him whole. It reminds me too much of the chair in Auggie's room. "It's the slowest night of the week at Rush. Everybody's broke and waiting for payday."

"Fair enough." My mind rolls memories of Bethany visiting Rush every Thursday night to get lit before heading here to fuck Auggie, and sometimes Robin too. I was always glad it was empty, except for the barflies and drunks who come in every night of the year. "Why am I here? Are you looking to replace my wife with me instead?"

Blushing, Robin has the decency to look mortified. "You're hot and all, and I wouldn't pass up the chance, but you're really not my type."

"And your type is?" I trail off, shifting on the tiny sofa, hating how it doesn't support my larger ass. I should be sitting on Auggie's throne instead of this silly toothpick-sized structure.

"The kind that has tits and a pussy– ya know, like your wife."

"Or the kind that's as tall as me, big as me, has a bigger schlong than me, but walks around with a guilty conscience the size of a newly forming planet?"

"Yeah, him too..." Robin shifts on the throne, looking mighty uncomfortable, and not physically. "About Auggie–"

"Don't!" I warn sternly in a tight voice. "I thought you guys were giving me a break so I wouldn't go fucking postal again. It's been such a pleasant four and a half days."

"Just listen, okay?" Unlike most people, I generally don't allow Robin to boss me around. It's one of the benefits of being his actual friend versus minion. But I decide to hear him out to be polite.

"Promise I won't have to deal with him tonight, and you can explain."

"No Auggie," Robin vows. "He's refusing to come home, remember?"

"Yeah, it was a pleasant surprise to see that the guy I cold-cocked in the nuts is sleeping on the other side of the wall from me."

"That's why you and I need to talk." Taking a deep breath, Rob gets real with me. Friendship, not manipulation. "Your wife has been helping Isis and Auggie, individually and together, so I need your help."

Of course, I get all melty inside, knowing someone needs me. I hate myself sometimes.

"I'm not chasing after them this time. I did what was necessary for our future happiness. Either they get with the program, or I'm done. So I'm just going to live my life, go about my business, and not kiss their asses anymore."

"Good luck with that." Chuckling sardonically, I give Robin a week tops before he breaks down and begs for their forgiveness.

"I'm being serious, Rory." Head hanging, Rob looks resolved yet disappointed. "I'm almost thirty. I'm done with their psychological warfare, emotional extortion, and borderline abusive behavior. But that doesn't mean I don't care about them anymore. So I'm going to fix things from afar while your wife fixes things up-close and personal."

"What do you mean?" Heart pounding uncontrollably, my guts twist so violently, I almost puke. "Beth's not fucking Auggie again, is she?"

"No!" Rob waves a dismissive hand in my face. "Christ, no. Bethany hated fucking Auggie. He turned into a nutjob during it. The one time Beth and I had actual fun, Auggie lost his shit. So, no, your wife will never touch Auggie sexually again, for her own sanity's sake."

"Okay, good," I mutter in relief, sagging against the ornate cushions.

"Are you against Bethany fucking anyone but you?" Rob asks out of curiosity, no judgement lacing his voice.

Rubbing at the back of my neck, I'm shocked by my own answer. "No, as long as I'm involved."

Face brightening with calculation, "Good," is all Robin has to say on that particular subject. "So Auggie is terrified he destroyed your friendship with that little stunt he pulled. He feels guilty, blaming himself. His ego is bruised worse than his nuts, and he agrees with the punishment."

"I don't– I flipped out, okay?" I plead with Robin. "I didn't mean to punch him in the nuts. I… I don't blame Auggie for me being bisexual, or for him touching me in a way that would show me what I was missing. Auggie didn't *force* me, and I did enjoy every second of it, but I never want a repeat. I just don't want to be his therapist anymore. If Auggie wants a friend, then we need to be friends. Not boss and minion, or landlord and tenant. No bullshit hanging over our heads. Just hang out and do friend shit."

"Good." Robin smiles slyly, then holds up his cellphone. "Don't get pissed at me, but I recorded your answer. Auggie wouldn't have believed you if you said that to his face, thinking you were being your usual too nice self. So I recorded you when you were your most honest."

"Are you fucking serious?" Growling, I can feel my face heating up with rage. "Goddamn you, Robin!"

"There." Robin sags against the throne, then tucks his phone into his pocket. "Sent. My good deed is done for the day. That's the last thing I needed to repair. Your friendship with Auggie will resume whenever you're ready."

"Is that all?" Relieved, I shift to stand from the sofa. "Why did we do this up here in the attic, and not in the living room? What's the big deal?"

"Now it's my turn to be your friend." Rob leans forward to pat my knee in a brotherly touch. "It's unlike you to go postal, Rory. Never seen that once in the decade we've known each other. You're the antithesis of violence."

"So," I mutter grumpily, crossing my arms over my chest, taking up a defensive position.

"I know Beth, bud," Rob has to go ahead and remind me how he knows my wife in the biblical sense. "She goes into bulldog mode for the ones she loves. But she's your wife, and it will come off as nagging behavior, where you won't digest what she's saying. It's what happens between Auggie, Isis, and me on a daily basis. Beth took over my *spouses*, so I'm dealing with hers."

"Oh," I drawl out, not liking this one bit.

"It's a fact of life. There's no way you'll listen to Beth, not completely. It's human nature to find it annoying, nagging, and want to avoid it at all costs. Trust me– *I know*."

"I don't look at Beth like that," I deny.

"Subconsciously, you do though... You're angry at yourself. Beth's said it to you, and she's said it to me, and now I'm going to repeat it. You're bi, Rory, and you shouldn't punish yourself because of it. Beth is too cerebral to allow you to tie yourself to her for life in a monogamous relationship, where you cut off half of what makes you who you are."

"Just because I'm bi doesn't mean I *need* to have sex with both guys and girls to be happy," I mutter defensively, feeling as if to do just that it shows I'm not in love enough with my wife.

"Who says?" Rob challenges me. "Who wrote that rule? Who says just because you're in a committed partnership, that sex means love? That sexual gratification erases the commitment, the affection, and the camaraderie you share with your partner? Who says you can't love more than one person at a time, without it erasing what you feel for either of them?"

"Rob, I didn't mean it like that." Faltering, I stumble over my words, because I know I've insulted Robin somehow, because he's in love with two people at the same time.

"Yes, you did," Rob brooks no room for argument. "Write your own rules. Make yourself happy, which will in turn make Bethany happy. God, I don't know how married couples survive. It feels like they get off on making their partner motherfucking miserable with their controlling, manipulative, abusive ego-trips and insecurities."

"Monogamy must work for some of us. Not everyone is built to share. It's no more or less enlightened."

"Yeah, like my parents," Rob points out. "They're blissfully happy, so are my aunt and uncle. But look around, Rory. The divorce rate is astronomical, with bitter wives and husbands getting off on hurting each other instead of loving each other, because they can't get off in the way they need."

"Jesus, when you paint the picture like that–"

"I am an artist, after all," Robin purrs smugly. "So don't follow rules that don't fit you. Don't make a problem where one isn't, because you think that's what you should be feeling. Guilt. Shame. The blame-game. You're a bisexual male who married a sexually evolved female specializing in the psychology of human sexuality."

"My wife is amazing," I murmur dreamily, pride infusing my voice.

"Who says just because you got married, the man goes to work, handing over his balls to his wife? In return, the wife hands her personality over to the husband. The wife lives the husband's life, never having one of her own. Right or wrong, she turns into a patronizing know-it-all, and he's suddenly a moron who gets mothered by his wife, because that's how society paints a marriage. She raises the kids while the dad has absolutely no ownership in how they are raised. Ya know, he's babysitting, not parenting. They screw twice a month under the cover of darkness to reaffirm their attractiveness, while the wife bitches at the husband for sneaking porn, and he ignores the hypocrisy as she drools over man-candy. The resentment, bitterness, insecurities, and power-struggle explodes one day when one of them cheats, breaking up a family that was doomed from the get-go due to following broken societal rules that are meant to oppress and depress females and emasculate males."

"Are you and Bethany besties now?" I rumble an uncomfortable laugh. "Wow, Rob. That diatribe came out of my wife's mouth no less than ten times in the past few months. I get it. Beth doesn't wash the dishes because she's a girl– she does it because she dirtied them. Now, if you could get Bethany to come to terms with the fact that me paying *our* bills doesn't make her a whore because she fucks me, I'd appreciate it."

"Beth and I enjoy each other's company, and I was the one who had her accepting tuition from you, Rory. She's helping me come to terms with the fact that I want to be a stay-at-home dad, no matter who's genetically the father. I just want to paint, take care of this house and our family, raise our children, and go to sleep between Auggie and Isis– that's all. There's no shame in it, no matter what society says about the man's role in life."

"Beth says everyone is to blame."

"She's right. We all just hop into the tiny boxes that were created for us, not questioning it one bit. Men treat women the way they do because they were taught to. Women treat men the way they do because they were taught to. As if we're completely different creatures, when we're not. The right thing– the brave thing –is to live this very short life by your own rules, being who you are, not living up to someone else's vision they have created for you."

"So, if I want to fuck someone, I should?" I try to follow Robin's logic, but it only leads to pain. "What about respect? Love? Commitment? Not rubbing your partner's face in your exploits?"

"What about mutual respect?" Robin volleys back. "Fidelity, respect, and love built in an unstifled, selfless environment, where each partner wants their partner to be happy and fulfilled, versus lowered to make them feel better about themselves. If I touch your arm, are we cheating together, when it's the same skin covering your dick? It's the reasons and emotions that makes it cheating."

"Fuck, dude. You sound beyond cynical– a whole 'nother world of bitter."

"It's not cynical– it's reality. Love is not romance. Romance is fantasy. Love is realistic. Marriages fail because it's a lifetime commitment you make every single day, not because your dick got hard and they gave you the warm and fuzzies. Marriage should be about forgiveness and understanding– friendship at its core. I'm speaking of negotiating, which you and Beth have done, not cheating. Fidelity isn't synonymous with monogamy, no matter what the thesaurus may say."

"So you brought me up here in the attic to fuck me?" Snorting, I sneer at Robin. "Sorry, bud, but you weren't on the negotiating table."

"That would be why I'm here." Devon manifests from the shadows, steps silent.

"Jesus Christ!" Arm raised to cover my face, as if I'm imagining this, I suck in several deep gasps of air. "How did I forget for one second that you're the least trustworthy person I've ever met? First you record me, now I find out you've had Devon eavesdropping this entire time."

"I'm of the school of thought where I do what's best for my friends, no matter if it's nefarious, illegal, or socially unacceptable." Robin flows to his feet, entirely unrepentant. "You can thank me later." Just before the door locks at his back, Rob calls to both Devon and me. "Thursday nights belong solely to you and your women from this night forward– make use of the gift."

"You come here looking for a hug?" My ice-breaker has Devon laughing at the ceiling, the carefree sound taking on a sinful note. Or maybe I think it's sinful because it arouses me, which is my problem, not Devon's. "Rob and Beth are right. I'm conflicted about my own nature."

"Truth?" Devon's more sober than usual. Not depressed or close to using, or acting high on life, the guy I used to know sits down on the throne. Not much smaller than Robin in stature, Devon looks powerful instead of ridiculous sitting in the wood and metal seat, even if his feet don't touch the floor.

"I've been looking forward to tonight all week," Devon reveals, shocking me senseless. "During Rob's sadistic version of hugging-it-out therapy on Monday, he told me to come back here tonight to help you out. I told you he said I had a friend in need, but didn't mention names. Anyway, the thought of tonight kept lowering my craving levels all week, giving me something to look forward to."

"I find it hard to believe you don't feel any guilt, not after how you behaved your entire teenage years."

"Truth, remember?" Devon shifts in the throne, drawing his legs up, then crossing them. Looking comfortable and at ease, I know he and I are on a different plane than we used to be. Real friendship, I guess.

"The thought of anyone touching Essie has murder plots playing out in my head. Sane? Probably not." Devon smirks deviously. "But then I see her insecurities glowing from her eyes, and remember how even the sex with me was tainted by bullshit. Will I ever give permission for Essie to fuck some random? Hell to the no, and I do mean permission. Essie and I are in a traditional marriage, where I wear the pants and she wears the apron, but out of respect, we both do all the duties as a team."

Trying to wrap my mind around that, "So you get to fool around with me, and call it therapy and friendship, while Essie sits at home with your baby growing in her belly?"

"I may be an asshole, but I do love Essie selflessly." Devon's glare would kill a lesser man. "Essie more than deserves a healthy sex life. There's a part of me that can never give that to her. I'm too fucked up, and my meds mess with my refractory period."

"You want me to fuck your wife?" All I receive in reply to that is a sinister eyebrow raise. "I know your junk works."

"For about a year, my dick shot five to ten times a day, but then the nightmare happened, and I couldn't get it up unless I was angry or terrified. The only release I had was during wet nightmares."

Sucking in a deep breath, I stop myself from offering comfort, knowing Devon would see it as pity. "How long?"

"You ask that as if somehow that has changed?" Devon mutters wryly. "Seven years. Women hit their sexual primes later in life. We're in ours now, and my dick may or may not function. It has a mind of its own. I thought Dr. Delaney wanted me to jerk off before I left the center to make sure the nightmares didn't incapacitate me. But that was only part of it. It's a miracle I function with the sheer volume of mood stabilizers flowing in my veins."

"But you do function, right?" I suddenly realize being hard doesn't equate to having the ability to ejaculate.

"I've gotten off twice since I got home, which in actuality means twice in like four or five months. The last time was when we conceived our baby. Once during the sadistic hugging session with Rob. Then he forced me to make love to Essie before I left, to make sure I functioned okay. But since, I've been in a nonstop state of arousal."

"Why not come then?" is followed by uncomfortable laughter bubbling up from my chest.

"Control. I love how powerful I feel when aroused, and I don't want to give that power away. I've gone down on Essie two or three times a day since Monday, getting off on it mentally and emotionally while denying myself sexual gratification. Plus, I was saving it up to make sure I could function for tonight with you."

"Oh, Christ!" Arching my back, I cover my face with my forearm. Struggling to erase the image Devon's words create in my mind, I focus on what else he's saying. "Control? What does that mean?"

"Losing control terrifies me," Devon admits like it kills him. "It's irrational, but I fear my meds won't work if I lose control during sex, and it will spill into other areas."

"That's not true, is it?" Heart aching, guts twisting, what I thought in my kitchen a few nights ago haunts me now. What if Devon can't even get a high off sex, when every other joy in life is out of the question?

"No, I'm just terrified." Raw with emotion, Devon shows me yet another facet of his personality. "I enjoy being hard, the longer the better. But when I finally get stimulation, it only takes thirty seconds to come. But the real problem is how it may be a good twenty-four hours before I can shoot again, no matter the need and want. Helluva refractory period."

"I have to get off this dinky sofa." Lunging to my feet, I begin pacing around the attic playroom. "Black and white facts that can't be misinterpreted, what do you want from me?"

"A friend. Sponsor. Someone I can talk to about anything, who won't judge me. Someone who's not related to me. Someone who has never harmed me or let me down. Someone who hasn't seen me at my lowest, and I don't just mean drugs. Someone to have fun with. Someone who will reaffirm my truth, how just because I'm not like everyone else doesn't make me abnormal or wrong. I'm just different."

"A lover?" I guess.

"Yeah, a lover. Someone who understands how both Essie and I feel. How I want to pleasure her, but she feels guilty, thinking I'm not getting anything out of it because I'm not physically getting off on it, when I am inside my head and heart. I don't want her to push me away, thinking it one-sided."

"So this–" I point around the attic. "Was your way of seducing me for your wife? Hell, Devon. We all know Essie makes me goddamn horny. No one will dispute that fact."

Head hitching backward, Devon releases that intoxicating laugh that never fails to smack me in the nuts. "Essie and I aren't compatible without lovers, and it's neither of our faults. It just is.

She needs to feel wanted, and she gets that feeling when the guy gets off. I can go down on her a billion times, and she won't believe I love every second of it. Even if my dick is hard, there's no guarantee cum will shoot."

"Essie needs *proof* that you're hot for her?" Jesus, can't this guy get a fucking break?

"Yeah. If I push my control, I might be able to prove it once a day at best, maybe a few times a week. But I know she'll pull away. I want to touch her, kiss her, go down on her– massage her all night long. But she wants to do those things to me too. Once my dick goes soft, it's soft. What woman would want to suck a flaccid cock, even if it felt amazing inside my head? She's not going to believe me, no matter what I say, after her past."

"Let me get this straight..." Feet halting, I come to a standstill in front of Devon as he owns the throne with his ass. "You're harder than hell, touching Essie for hours, but you won't let her touch you back, because you're saving your erection for sex, but you only last like thirty seconds once you get stimulated? Then you're out of commission for like a day because of your meds?"

"Yeah, that's the gist of it." Devon smirks up at me. "Most of it anyway. Sure, I'd love her to stroke my dick and rub my body, but it gets me too hot and I'll shoot and be worthless for the main event."

"I'm gonna teach you how to edge." Now it's my turn to grin. I'm blessed with a refractory period of less than five minutes, but I love nothing more than building tension, addicted to the insane pressure in my dick.

"Edge?" Devon pops a brow in disbelief, not thinking I can help.

"Edging. Dev, your dick is stuck at fourteen, where you get off as quickly as possible before you get caught. It will take a while, but you'll eventually be able to be stimulated for as long as you want and not come until you're ready. Mouth. Hands. Pussy. Ass. You can be as savage as you need to be without going off."

Clearing his throat, Devon adjusts his junk while shifting in his seat. "Yeah, teach me that... please."

"What's this between us mean?" Pointing back and forth between us, I'm terrified of what answer Devon may provide.

"Do you ever hold back from Beth because you're worried you'll either hurt her feelings, or she'll judge you? Like you can't say or do certain things with her because you fear how she'll take it, because her opinion of you matters more than everything. So it's so goddamn stressful, you swallow whatever it was you wish you could tell her?"

"Yeah," I breathe, feeling Devon on every level. "All the time. I don't want to disappoint her."

"That won't ever come between us." Now Devon's pointing at me, then him. "If I look like a fool, or nuts, or a sick fuck, you won't care. You'll either say yes or no, then let it go. Maybe talk me down from the ledge if my meds aren't working right and my idea is very, *very* bad."

"Do you even like guys?" Confused, Devon's answer is important.

"I like to have fun." Devon flows from the throne like water, knees landing on the floor as silently as he walks. Dark eyes glow up at me through the lace of his lashes, cheeks pink with lust. "I'm not your submissive," Devon stresses, palms sliding up my thighs.

Frozen, all I can do is swallow as I gaze down at Devon, instinctively knowing what comes next. "You are the most powerful, commanding, psychotic motherfucker I've ever met, Devon."

"Just making sure you remember that fact while I'm on my knees." Small fingers tug down my zipper, revealing the navy fabric of my boxers.

"And this is fun for you?" I don't say sucking dick, because I don't want Devon to stop, thinking this emasculating.

Rolling his eyes, Devon yet again reads my thoughts. "Even while on my knees, I'm going to delve deep inside your head and blow your mind." A single fingertip rubs the strip of fabric revealed by my open fly, stimulating my dick. "Fun for me has a different connotation than it does to everyone else. I've had to adapt to *feel* what others take so easily for granted."

Tremors rolling up and down my spine, all I can do is stare down at Devon in wonder, knowing he doesn't make himself vulnerable like this with too many people. A large part of me is aroused beyond measure, while a small part feels honored– it's that kernel that terrifies me, knowing there is nothing casual about this encounter.

"Seventy years," Devon murmurs, breath warming me through my boxers. A tentative lick has my knees weakening, boxers dampening with hot saliva. Teeth set into my dick, a hand supports my ass to keep me from falling backward. "I wasn't seducing you for Essie, by the way… this was all for me."

"Fuck…" propels out of me in a gush as Devon's tongue slides up two inches of my dick. Fingertips pull more of my boxers away, then teeth scrape against my sensitive flesh. What should hurt has my mind spinning until I'm a few seconds away from fainting.

"Breathe," Devon warns, fingers popping the button on my jeans. Just like when we were kids, I follow his lead. *Breathe.* Hooking into my belt loops, my pants are tugged past my hips, boxers joining the ride. Leaning away, Dev orders, "Kick your sneakers and jeans off– shirt too. I want every inch of your goddamn body touching mine."

In a blink, my clothing disintegrates, and for once I feel no shame or guilt. Standing on shaky legs, I glance at the sofa in question. I hated it earlier, but now I need the support.

"Not yet." Warm palms slide up and down my thighs, getting a scant inch from my hanging sack. Fingertips play with the fuzzy hair on my legs, carding through it, nails scratching at my skin. "I'm a giver," Devon warns.

"So am I," I warn back how I'm going to touch Devon long after his cock deflates.

Giant dark eyes glaze over, pupils blown. Body visually vibrating, Devon moans, back arching with a shudder. "I'm about to bring the fun."

"Do it!" I order, not caring that it will piss the alpha male off. My cock's pounding so hard, it's tapping my belly. "Prove you love sucking dick– suck me."

"I'm not fragile," Devon challenges me back. "Palm my skull, pull my hair, and move your hips. Be a giver, not a pussy."

Lashing out quicker than a snake's strike, Devon deep throats my dick on the first pass, swallowing me down his throat.

Fingernails dig into my ass, keeping me upright. "Ugh!" Grunt after grunt, Devon has his version of fun– it's so fucking good, it's torture. My nature rears its head as I try to be gentle in thanks for sucking my dick.

Flesh slipping out of his mouth, "You're not my first dick," Devon admits, and it makes me harder for some bizarre reason. Hands snare mine, then force them onto the top of his head. "The first guy used gaslighting to make me think my rape was my idea. But he was gentle about it, which was a bigger head-trip than the rape. The second guy was fun, but he was innocent– you're not."

I give Devon what he wants, because it's better than getting angry over what happened to him. I'm not a violent person by nature, but if Devon's attacker still lived, I'd bury him.

"Harder," I moan, drawing Devon's mouth over my dick, using his hair as a handhold. Hips swaying in a counterthrust to Devon's movements, we both work at giving me pleasure. "More of that," I praise, fingernails digging into his scalp. "Not gonna last long."

Sinful laughter reverberates around my dick, Devon is most certainly having his brand of fun. Just as I get near the edge, he leans backward, causing my dick to slap him in the chin. Palms press against my hips, shoving me backward onto the fragile sofa.

Sprawling, I fear breaking the furniture with my big body. "You're going to teach me to last longer by edging, but you're a one-pump chump?" Devon taunts me as he kneels between my spread thighs.

Eyes hypnotically snare mine and I can't look away. "I've had exactly one blowjob before tonight from a guy. I'm not gonna lie– he's the most skilled cocksucker known to man. But I didn't want him like that. You?" Reaching down, I caress the side of Devon's neck softly, curling my fingers around to the nape. "It'll take a miracle to last." While Devon's left reeling, I wrap my fingers into his hair, then shove his head against my crotch. "Suck it. Drink it. Swallow it. Don't miss a drop."

"*Oh, God.*" Devon writhes, moaning uncontrollably, and I learn a person can in fact get off inside their head and not have it come out of their dick. I knew nothing would prepare me for Devon writhing under or above me.

A lick. A suck. A kiss to the head of my dick. The subtle scrape of teeth as a hot mouth wraps around my flesh. It's less than a second, I bump the back of Devon's throat, and I'm shouting my release to the ceiling, hairs snapping off in my fist.

Falling back against the sofa, panting like I just ran a marathon, I blink repeatedly to clear my vision. As my eyes crack open, I spy Devon smirking the naughtiest, dirtiest of smirks.

"Did I bring the fun?" Voice playful, Devon can't hide the warble of vulnerability that seeps through.

Refusing to pretend this is casual, I do something I've never done before but have always wanted to try, because it's not something I do with casual conquests. Hand lashing out, my fingers wrap around the front of Devon's neck. Drawing him up, the sensation of his swallowing against my palm is sexual enough to almost bring my dick back to life thirty seconds after I got off.

"Bring it on," I breathe against Devon's mouth. Hesitating, I check his body language, finding blown pupils and lips damp with my cum. Bridging the gap, we kiss. I've never kissed another dude, and I instinctively know it's far too intimate of an act that Devon never has either.

Moaning, rubbing his clothed body against mine, Devon slips his tongue past my lips. The flavor of my cum explodes on my taste buds, causing all the blood in my body to flood south.

"I don't know if I should be jealous or flattered." Devon palms my cock, stroking lightly because I'm still too sensitive. "Flattered, because I get to play with your fat cock."

"Too many clothes." Voice breathy, my fingers tear at Devon's t-shirt. "Need to give you that hug and show you how to edge– want you to come in my hand."

"Gonna come in my pants if we don't hurry the hell up." Struggling, peals of laughter flow from Devon's arched throat, and it's the hottest goddamn sound I've ever heard. "I've been edging since Monday, you sadist."

Leaning forward, I don't know which I want more– to get the fucking t-shirt off Devon's lean chest, or suck on his throat. I try for both, and end up choking us both with the shirt.

"I'm so fucking glad you're wearing sweats." Hands diving deep, I find out why Devon's cock was outlined perfectly in Jersey cotton. "No shorts."

"I'd live in sweats and no boxers if I could get away with it at work." Pants tossed across the attic, Devon crawls on top of me, pushing me flat against the sofa. He's taking charge again. "I've learned scratchy, unforgiving fabrics, zippers, buttons, elastic, and waistbands exacerbate my tactile issues."

"What about flesh on flesh?" Raising an eyebrow, I taunt Devon.

Releasing that amazing sound again, Devon's flying high. "We're about to find out." After maneuvering me around on the sofa where he wants me, Devon turns into my little spoon. "So many options. Decided this would be a good starting point. You can hug and tug, but we'll have to wrench our necks a bit to kiss."

"Thank God," I murmur in relief as I tuck Devon close to my body. "I was scared you wouldn't be into kissing."

"Kissing isn't masculine or feminine." Devon wiggles, purposefully wedging my hard-on between his ass cheeks. *God!* "It just feels incredible."

"Don't freak out if I end up jizzing in your ass crack." Wrapping my arms tightly around Devon, words can't even describe how this feels.

"Wouldn't be the first time," Devon murmurs softly, spiraling somewhere he shouldn't go. "But it'd be the first time I wanted it."

"Won't be the last either, then." Lips latched onto his neck, throat convulsing as I suck, I reach around to grab Devon's dick. Searing hot, the dang thing has a pulse of its own. "Stop abusing your dick and get it off once in a while, you control freak."

"Not gonna last ten seconds at this rate," Devon warns through clenched teeth as his spine bows against me.

"If you're going to shoot, squeeze my wrist, and I'll back off." Hand loosely cupping his flesh, I allow the shaft to slide up and down through my curled fingers, not stimulating him enough to get off. The feel of fingers tightening around my wrist shocks me. "Already?" I back off, cupping his heavy balls instead.

"I warned you," Devon hisses, neck arching beneath my lips. "The struggle is real."

"The struggle feels good– for both of us." Closing my eyes, I sink into the sensation of a warm body curled into mine, a hard dick sliding between my fingers, and scratchy hair tickling the inside of my wrist. "I'm bi. No turning back now."

The combination of Devon's laughter and the way his butt cheeks tighten around my shaft has me on the brink of coming already. So much for teaching Devon a lesson, when I can't even last.

Over the next few minutes, I hold a writhing body, backing off every time fingertips dig into my wrist. We're building more than friendship here– trust. Trust flows back and forth. Devon trusting me to stop, and me trusting Devon to alert me. The more times we hit the edge and back off, the stronger our bond is that forms.

"It's not going away anymore," Devon warns, panting breathlessly. "It's gonna come out on its own."

"That'll happen years from now, no matter how much you train your dick– enjoy it." Moaning, I'm enjoying myself too much. "Jesus, Devon. I can feel your bud rubbing against my dick. You don't even need to squeeze my wrist anymore– your asshole clenches in warning."

"Oh. My. God!" Devon writhes, a heartbeat away from losing it. "Don't talk like that unless you want my cum coating your hand."

"I do," I admit without shame or guilt. "I want nothing more than you writhing against me."

"I'm scared," Devon whispers, the most vulnerable I've ever heard him.

"Don't be."

"What if I lose control?"

"That's the point, isn't it?"

"What if I can't get it back?"

"I'm six-foot-four and two hundred and thirty pounds. You need to trust me enough to know I'll stop you, no matter what. I'll keep you safe." Hips rock against me, simultaneously sliding a hard dick through my fist while cushioning mine between his ass cheeks. "Let go, and know I'll take care of your control while you do. When you're ready, I'll give it back to you."

"Rory!" Terror laces Devon's shout of ecstasy, flesh jerking in my hand, but he refuses to come.

"Let go– don't stop yourself. Let it roll over you. Don't feel ashamed you couldn't stop it. Don't be afraid you'll lose control. I want you to lose control– I'll get off on it. Then it'll feel amazing to give it back to you." Chanting, coaxing, I'm no longer jerking Devon off or rocking my hips. I let him take control, give him the power to reach for his own orgasm.

"I trust you." One more rock of his hips, and I learn exactly what Devon Mason looks like when he's free. The glorious sight brings tears to my eyes, over-shadowing the pleasure I experience as I dampen his ass with my cum.

Melting against me, Devon vibrates in my arms, like he's forcing his muscles to stop quivering. "Stand up," I order, and I'm shocked when he does as I bid. I own him right now, and he's trusting me not to abuse the power. As he comes down, I'll let him take the lead again.

Shifting on the sofa, I part my legs and move Devon to stand between my knees, supporting him. "My legs are jittery." He laughs at himself, showing me how badly his hands are shaking.

Moaning, I finally take the opportunity to check Devon out from head to toe. "You have one helluva tight body– *fuck!*" Five and a half foot of tan skin covering corded muscles with a sparse smattering of wiry hair. My eyes are torn in indecision, between wanting to stare at his flat nipples or his satisfied junk. "Your dick makes my mouth water." Hanging loose, glossy with cum, with the heavy sack swinging between his muscular thighs.

Devon reaches forward, snagging my wrist. My palm is brought up to my mouth. "Lick," he demands, grabbing for his iron-clad control. "I want to watch you suck my cum off your fingers."

Proving Devon's trust in me wasn't misplaced, I give up control. Heart hammering, if I could get off again, hearing those filthy words in Devon's husky voice would have done it. Obeying, guttural groans flee my mouth as I roll Devon's taste around my tongue– savoring it.

"Have you ever sucked dick before?" Devon's question has me blinking, coming awake. "I won't get hard, but it would be easier to learn on a soft cock– no chance of choking. We have a lot we can teach each other."

Devon's earlier words flow through my mind, how he wants Essie to believe him when he says he wants touch, whether he's hard or soft. Other than being penetrated, you can do a lot with a soft cock.

Groaning around the invasion, my lips suck at the loose flesh, drawing all of his junk into my mouth, balls and all. Trusting me, Devon collapses, curling his chest to rest against the top of my head as I feast between his hips. Arms fold over my shoulders, muffling Devon's cries of surrender.

Part of me wishes I could get hard again so I could get off again, but the larger part wants to experience what Devon does on a daily basis. The need for pleasure but your junk doesn't match up with the signals firing in your brain.

My body lights up like a livewire, vibrating with an energy I don't recognize. Sucking at Devon's soft dick and sack, I allow them to fall from my lips. Then I nudge it out of my way, burying my face in the juncture between his thigh and junk. Sucking, licking, biting at anything I can reach, I struggle to stay upright as Devon writhes over top of me.

"I love being touched– I know how fucking insane that sounds coming from the guy who is terrified of being touched, but I do. I need it."

"You trust me," I mutter with conviction. "That's the difference. I'll show Essie you can trust her too."

Legs part, foot coming to rest on the sofa cushion next to my hip. Devon gives me access to darker, deeper places. Tongue delving deep, I taste my own cum splattered against his flesh.

"I'm gonna come," Devon warns in a throaty moan, and I learn how amazingly complex the man riding my face is. "Oh, my God, Rory! It's more intense than the last time. Your tongue, don't stop."

Scratching my back and biting the top of my head, Devon climaxes without ejaculating. Mind taking over to offer an outlet his body can't provide, he evolves past what the rest of us see as normal. The end goal for a guy is always ejaculating. Devon just debunked that myth, and a tinge of jealousy overpowers me.

Sucking at his taint while trying to tongue the writhing man's asshole, I let go. I can't get hard, but I experience a small sliver of the pleasure Devon's riding.

"Nothing has ever felt... so... fucking... good..." Devon takes the words right out of my head, collapsing over top of me, taking me down on the sofa too. "We need a nap now."

Laughing, I alligator roll us on the sofa until we're comfortable, then immediately close my eyes. "Gonna be super late for work."

"You don't care," Devon murmurs against the side of my throat. "Be bad, Rory. Life's more fun when you're bad."

"How fast did the Charger go?" I ask on a hunch.

Slurring dreamily, "I got her up to one-twenty-four. She's a helluva lot faster than the Camaro. Ozzy got hard when I let him take her for a spin, and everyone poured out of the houses when I brought her home. She's well-loved."

"Which road?" Smirking, I try to keep the amusement out of my voice.

"On Mulholland, between Deforest and Pine, there's a beautiful straight stretch, but it's only a mile or so. I had to slow it down before the road dipped."

"That Hellcat is a real beauty– I got your machine to hit one-sixty-seven before I pussied out," I murmur smugly.

"Where the hell did you find a stretch of road long enough to safely hit that speed and then slow back down again?" The cop in Devon erupts, either that or it's his concern for me.

Biting my lip, I smother a snicker. "Next time, we'll just hit the speedway."

"Dick!" Devon punches me in the arm, pulling his hit. "You test-drive cars at the goddamn speedway?"

"Sometimes it pays to be a good guy, Devon... because no one expects it when you're actually being bad."

CHAPTER NINE

"You're bizarrely relaxed," Isis comments as she slides into the booth bench opposite me. Even for a Thursday night, it's dead in here. Usually there's an influx an hour or so before closing. We pick up customers who work third shift at the local manufacturing plant, then pick up their fellow employees who are on their way home after second shift.

"You're freakishly calm," I volley back, surprised to see Isis calm when she's usually taut like a frayed string ready to snap.

"Carrie said you were four hours late tonight." Isis raises a manicured eyebrow, waiting patiently for once. "I was here and you weren't."

"Is there a question in there somewhere?" I tease. Chuckles bubble up as Isis starts to crack. "Yeah, I was late. Devon and I have been hanging out lately. Essie and Beth thought it would be a good idea."

"Yeah, but…" Her tiny heart-shaped face twists up in confusion. "You look like you just got laid by fifty supermodels at a sex toy tradeshow." Seconds count down, where I don't respond to her passive-aggressive way of asking if Devon and I are messing around. If Isis asks, I'll answer. But this is a non-question.

Taking my nonresponse as a *back off*, "Okay, it's none of my business. As long as you're happy and relaxed, and you do look good tonight." Isis fiddles with a cocktail napkin I snagged when Carrie gave me a Coke. "Devon let me touch his new car."

Laughing, I take a slug of my drink. "Don't even think about touching my lady." Rush is an old warehouse surrounded by a sea of parking lot. Just before I bought the Challenger, I erected a pole barn as a garage to store my car, tools, and toys. No matter who lived inside Rush, none of them had access to my garage—

except for Bethany now. But I park my wife's car in there for her, tucking it in for the night.

"Dev wouldn't let me drive it, though." Isis pouts. Being raised with the Pussy Magnet as the family car skewed her view on transportation. Isis paid a mint for her sporty little MX-5 Miata. I built her a carport off the side of my pole barn for it.

"How's pregnancy treating you?" Tilting my chin, I gesture to the orange juice she's nursing.

My best friend and business partner reveals herself. "I'm scared," and I can suddenly see the resemblance between the aunt and nephew.

"Do you know the one thing Rob would never do?" I coax, trying to alleviate her fear. "Harm you. What happened with the last baby was nature. You're going to be okay, Isis. You're going to be a great mom, and Robin is going to be an amazing father."

"It's Auggie's spawn." Isis drains her glass dry.

"Robin made the kid with Auggie's baby juice." Chuckling, the lengths that bastard goes to… "Don't know how he managed it, but I'd say that makes the baby just as much his, don't you?"

"I can't be around Robin right now." Isis stares down at her hands, acting so unlike the Isis who rules the world. Reaching forward, I rest my palm over her hands, then squeeze slightly. We don't touch much, but Isis is a Mason, and I've learned a few things about Masons this week. As I suspected, the tears spring to her eyes, and the truth tumbles out.

"But you want to be." No question needed. Isis is just as obsessed with Robin as he is with her. Robin is the glue in this fucked up sandwich, with both Auggie and Isis in love with him and Rob in love with them, with Auggie and Isis having a power-struggle, love-hate relationship.

Watery dark eyes peer up at me through damp lashes, imploring me to make it all better. I was the one who held Isis in the hospital, tried to entertain her the best I could, then curled around her as she slept once she came back home here at Rush.

"I'm so scared, Rory." Isis's admission guts me.

Before I can react or respond, movement catches my eye. Auggie steps away from the bar, which goes to show how distracted I've been. Two shots are placed in front of me, then a pair of large hands rub the nape of my neck and shoulders– an apology and thank you all rolled into one.

Those same hands curl under a crying Isis's armpits, then lift her from the booth. Once she's on her feet, Auggie tucks Isis to his chest, arms wrapping around her tightly. They slowly walk from the bar area, down the hallway, then disappear up the staircase to our apartments.

I'd do anything I could to fix them, make them happy and healthy, but Beth's right– I can't. I've got to let them go. Let them either fix it or fuck it up more. Isis and Auggie need to bond right now, and the comfort Isis is seeking has to come from her men.

Breaking the rules slightly, I tap out a quick text to Robin.

–Isis is breaking down and Auggie isn't much better. Get your ass over here and comfort them both.

Not expecting a reply, I nurse the shot of scotch. "Mmm… Auggie must really be sorry," I muse to myself. "He poured from the only bottle of Lagavulin." Taking another tiny sip, enjoying the smoky note hitting my tongue, "Thank you, Auggie."

Not two and a half minutes later, Robin's briskly walking through Rush, not acknowledging anyone on his way by. Either he broke the sound barrier driving from the Spook House, or he was at his studio on Main Street and he drove like a bat outta hell to get here.

Halfway through my second shot, feeling nice and toasty, I spot my wife dragging her bag of tricks toward me. "Little pup." With a grin, I salute her with my shot glass.

"Interesting." Beth drops the heavy bag on her side of the booth with a groan of pleasure. Then she makes a beeline to the bar. Carrie already announced last call and turned up the house lights, but Beth doesn't count. My woman hops over the bar, which tells me she had started drinking during her study session and had to stop in order to drive home.

"Tomorrow's Friday," Bethany announces, plopping a bottle of Patrón on the tabletop, followed by a container of limes and a salt shaker. "No school for three whole days. Woot!" She pulls a shot glass out of her bra.

"Rough study session?" Amused, I watch my wife like she's the most fascinating human in all of creation. "Studying serial rapists getting you down?"

"I had an awesome night." Bethany's wide-eyed and bushytailed, putting down two shots in quick succession. "My advisor read over my outline for **P & L**'s case study, and *loved* it!" Another shot, followed by a wedge of lime. "We didn't drink and play games. Daniel Holtzclaw's case was too interesting– he's a cop, you know?"

I don't know– have absolutely no clue what Bethany's talking about.

"Calling it a night, boss." Carrie waves on her way by, chuckling at my wife as she goes. I finally take note Rush is empty except for us. My bartender turns the house lights back down to an intimate level, then locks us up in here nice and tight.

"If you weren't drinking tonight, how the hell are you so lit?" Beth's always a trip when she's drunk– horny, crazy, and amusing.

"Oh!" Beth makes a dismissive sound, rolls her eyes, and waves her hand in the air like it's nothing at all. "Rob pulled up beside me in the parking lot, got out, took two hits off a joint, then gave it to me."

"So you smoked it?" Biting my lip, I barely suppress my laughter.

"What was I supposed to do, throw it away?" Beth looks insulted, staring me down as she pours herself another shot. Grumpy, thinking I'm judging her. "That would be an insult to Mary Prynne."

"Rob offers me pot just about every single day," I admit, sucking back the last of the Lagavulin. Hopping up from the bench, I slip into the DJ booth and select some hardcore heavy metal, leaving it at a level where I can still hear Bethany without screaming.

Beth's work week is just ending, but mine's just beginning. One of the advantages of managing a club is the fact that I don't go to work until late in the day and can push the clerical bullshit off onto Isis. So I can get blitzed and sleep it off way before I have to be at work. One of the disadvantages, pounding music and the smell of alcohol exacerbate a hangover.

Abruptly pulling my wife from the booth, I chuckle at the shriek she releases. "No one can hear you scream, little girl," I warn against the side of her neck, hot breath beading gooseflesh across her skin.

"What do you do?" Beth's question confuses the piss outta me.

"Do about what?" After licking my forearm to make it wet, I shake salt all over it. "Open," I command, and wonder what it's like to be Devon. Everyone does as he says, and his wife is his little zealot. Mine… surprisingly she opens her mouth, but it's to ask more questions.

"When Rob shares his weed?" No judgement, just curiosity, which is why I love my wife.

"I don't look a gift-horse in the mouth, lil pup– I smoke the hell out of it." Raising my forearm to her lips, "Open," I command again.

Pink tongue hot against my skin, Beth makes my knees go weak with the salacious way she licks the salt. Squishing her face up, lips pucker, "Uuugghhh…" Bethany shudders from the salt hitting her taste buds. "Hurry!"

"Open," I order again, refusing to hand her a shot glass. Giggling like a fiend, I pour tequila straight from the bottle into her upraised, open mouth. Three swallows later, I insert a lime wedge. "Give it ten minutes before you attempt anymore. I'm not carrying your ass upstairs."

With a long lick, I clean the rest of the salt off my arm, then guzzle straight from the bottle, forgoing the lime because that's not my thing.

Smiling like the Cheshire cat, "Kiss me," Beth murmurs from around the lime wedge, like the green rind is a row of her teeth. "Kiss my lips, babe."

Laughing hysterically, there's no way in hell I'm going to kiss Beth with that lime wedge in her mouth.

Grinning bigger, "C'mon, babe– kiss my lips." Bethany's giggling so hard, she has to keep biting the lime or else she'd drop it. "Kiss me. Ya know you wanna."

"Don't drop it," I warn, upending Bethany and tossing her over my shoulder. "Drop the lime and I'll make you eat the whole container." I flop her ass on the bar.

Drunk and high, Beth keeps repeating, "Kiss my lips, babe," reminiscent of when she was singing *weee... weee... weee* like the Geico Pig last time she was drunk around me.

"Oh, I'm going to kiss your lips, but don't drop the lime," I warn again, pressing the wedge up against her teeth. "No dropsies."

Giggling while trying to head-bang to Slipknot and not drop her lime, Bethany doesn't stop me as I tug her jeans off. "Still sore? Let's check out that fresh wax job... and I'm more than curious to see if your asshole looks any different than last night."

Jeans tossed in the direction of our booth, I place first one, then the other foot on the bar, spreading my wife open like an all-you-can-eat buffet. "Mmm... beautiful," I murmur in awe, fingers spreading her cheeks apart to peek at her rosebud. Disappointed, I whine, "Aahh... it doesn't look any different."

"What were you expecting?" Beth sits up, using only her stomach muscles, proving she's a champion at crunches. "An asshole is an asshole is an asshole."

"Don't drop your lime," I remind her, pressing it farther into her mouth. "Not all assholes are created equal." Some are hairy, and some are waxed and bleached. Remembering the reaction I got from licking an asshole earlier, I'm curious to see what Bethany will do– after all, she bleached it for me, right?

"Ah! I dropped my lime!" is not the reaction I expected. "Shit, I need another one. Hey– where are you going? I thought you were gonna toss my salad?"

Chuckling nonstop, I plunk the container of lime wedges an inch from Beth's face. "I think we're gonna need all of these, don't you?" Beth's giggles have her wiggling all over the bar. "Behave, or else I'll reach over and grab the lemons next."

"Oh, no." Beth pops another lime wedge into her mouth.

"The olives."

"No." ... and another one.

"Cocktail onion." I lower my face to Beth's pussy, admiring the beautiful wax job Essie did. Not a stray hair in sight, and no redness or bumps. Just a smooth landscape of pink, lickable flesh.

Bethany tries to shove a third wedge into her mouth, but fails.

"Maraschino cherries?"

Limes fly everywhere as Bethany spits them out. "Yes, sir." Spreading her legs wider, Beth opens her mouth and waits for her treat.

Reaching over the bar, I snag the cherries. Grinning naughtily, I rub the cherry along Beth's slit, causing her to writhe in a wanton rhythm. As added torment, I swirl around her nub, then shove it into her, only to pull it back out an instant later.

"I should put my cock in your mouth instead, don't you think?" Smirking down at my wife, I pop the cherry coated in pussy juice into her mouth. She immediately tries to tie the stem with her tongue, showing me the skills she'll use on my cock.

"Mmm... good girl."

I'd love to think I haven't been going through an existential crisis for the past few months. My payment for marrying Bethany turned my world upside down. Realizing marriage wasn't what I saw in the movies was a cold splash of reality as Beth and I found our common ground. My blowup at my best friends had me rethinking who I was at my core. Then add this week with Devon...

So I expect to feel different as my tongue dives deep inside my wife's pussy, like after sucking dick tonight, I'll suddenly not enjoy it. Groaning, Beth tastes just as intoxicating as she did last night, affecting my cock just as much.

Humming in appreciation, satisfaction roils through my bloodstream as Bethany goes wild on top of the bar, screaming my name and yanking my hair, pushing my face closer to her pussy. I could come just listening to her come, but I'm all about the edge.

"Rory!" Bethany grumbles in frustration as I flip her around on the bar, until she's on all fours, then I crawl up behind her.

"Eat your cherries, lil pup," I order, handing her another one. "Take your medicine."

"You administering Peckercillin, babe?" Bethany lowers her shoulders, raising her ass, then she wiggles suggestively in front of my face. "I sure could use a dose."

"Good God, I love you," eclipses the sound of my zipper lowering. It's a struggle, but I manage to get my hard cock out of my pants. I have a feeling the more sex I have, the more I'm going to want, and I'm going to be getting a lot of sex in the immediate future.

Groaning together, my eyes roll into the back of my head as Beth's pussy wraps around my dick. The hot, silky sheath forms a tight fist, milking me with every thrust. Beth loses all lucidity as I pump her harder than usual, speared on by the strange energy I've felt all night.

"Do you wanna know what I did tonight, lil pup?" Hands cupping Bethany's breasts, I raise her up onto her knees, with her back to my chest. "Hmm?"

Arching her neck, Beth rocks her hips, fucking herself on my cock. "Jesus, you feel thick tonight."

Part of me is testing her, but the rest of me knows exactly how she'll react. "Devon knelt on the attic floor in the Spook House, looked up at me with those gigantic blue eyes of his... so dark and infinite. Then he unzipped my pants and sucked my cock dry."

"Oh, God!" Bethany cries out, body quivering, pussy clenching around my cock.

"I didn't wash my dick, Beth–"

"Rory!" Shuddering violently, Beth slips from my hands to rest her elbows on the bar.

"Then I jerked him off," I chant, timing my words with my thrusts. All the edging in the world isn't going to stop me from coming inside my wife, not with the way her pussy is violently clenching me. "Devon ordered me to lick his cum off my hand."

"You did it, didn't you?" Not an accusation, but a breathy wish.

"Yeah, and I loved every second of it." Thrusting harder, I can't help but moan loud enough it's heard over the sound system. "So I sucked Devon's cock."

Losing the ability of coherent speech, Bethany releases a string of nonsensical words as she writhes all over the bar. Unable to not answer the siren call of a climaxing pussy, I come in jerky starts and stops, uttering gibberish myself.

Collapsing to the bar in a puddle of satisfied limbs, Bethany and I are woven together like a pretzel. Drowsy, I slur, "Should I feel guilty?"

Beth tries to speak, but ends up clearing her throat for a few seconds first. "Just imagining it had me coming all over you. Someday I hope you and Devon trust us enough to let me and Essie watch you together."

"I'll take that as a no." I chuckle, because Beth's experiencing wicked aftershocks. "I feel guilty that I don't feel guilty." Pausing, I decide I trust Beth enough to understand how I'm feeling. "It's not casual for me, and I don't think it is for him either."

"Devon's demisexual, Rory." Beth curls around my body, holding me tight. "If he came for you willingly, then he has a strong emotional connection to you."

"What?" I whisper, shocked stupid.

"Not gonna lie– Essie, Rob, and I have been talking about this all week, since Devon shared his journal with us. I doubt he'll share it with you, because he'll probably tell you in person, which is more intimate. We knew he'd crave touching you, sucking you, but we weren't sure he'd allow you to reciprocate. Was Devon okay?"

"I'm a bit… gobsmacked right now, Beth." Taking a deep breath, I try to get my equilibrium. "Devon ejaculated in my hand. He kept talking about wanting Essie to touch him, but he feared she'd stop once he came and couldn't get hard again. He wants her to touch him anyway. So I took that knowledge and sucked him off, even though he was soft– ate him out too. Devon's orgasm was the most transcendental experience of my entire life. He *came* without ejaculating– from inside his head."

"Good." Beth releases all of her muscles at once, deflating in relief. "To be inside Devon's mind is a scary place, so I feared he couldn't have a fulfilling sexual existence. But he can, and that's all that matters. None of us care how Devon gets gratification as long as he does."

"So you did pimp me out?" I accuse, too tired and replete to get angry.

"Rory, you're grasping at straws, getting angry at something because you're feeling emotionally uncomfortable. You care about Devon. You got off with him, on him, and in him. Now you're confused because you're in love with me, just had sex with me and loved every minute of it, so how can you possibly care about Devon too, right? You're also wondering why I was turned on by it, then relieved because of it, instead of turning into a jealous, spiteful, hurt mess."

"Get outta my head, woman," I tease, squeezing her tight. Stretching, I decide, while the bar is a great place to fuck on, it's not the best place to cuddle. "Can you carry me upstairs?"

Giggling, Beth's tits jiggle against my arms. "Do you smell smoke?"

"You're a pot hound now, aren't ya?" Taking a few sniffs, I realize she's right. "C'mon out, ya creepy ass voyeur."

"Anyone care for a post-coital smoke?" Robin reveals himself, stepping away from the far end of the bar, joint cherry glowing in the shadows as he takes another hit.

"How long have you been watching?" I accuse, not getting too upset about it. Robin was in the same hotel room when I lost my virginity. He's fucked my wife, and watched her in every sexual position known to man in the Playroom.

"Sharing is caring." A joint is placed between my lips. As soon as I take a deep draw, it's back in its rightful place, with Robin sucking it down. "Auggie and Isis are sleeping, so when Slipknot poured through the sound system, I thought I'd investigate."

"What's so odd about Slipknot?" Beth struggles to sit up, not giving a shit that she's only wearing a t-shirt covered in cocktail garnishes and jizz. Reaching up, she plucks the joint out of Robin's mouth, then takes a hit.

Instead of turning pissy, like he would with anyone else, Rob flashes Bethany a lascivious look. Puckering up, he waits for his three a.m. snack to return to his welcoming embrace.

After successfully executing a perfect series of smoke rings, Rob answers Beth's question. "Our boy lost his v-card after junior prom."

"That's not that bizarre." Beth grins at me, all proud like– totally fucking high out of her gourd.

"*My* junior prom," Robin stresses, causing me to bark a laugh. "Hotel party afterward– Slipknot was playing." He pats my shoulder like a proud papa. "So we had this little game. Every time Rory was close to scoring with a chick, we'd put on Slipknot."

"So you played it tonight?" Beth squints at me, confused.

"Oh, our boy's played it more than just tonight for you, lover." Rob rubs Bethany's thigh, and I don't get too bent out of shape, because I'll leave it to her to swat him away. Then I realize Rob's playing in the cum trailing down the inside of her thigh. "So when I heard Slipknot, I had to investigate."

"Hmm..." Beth and I watch wide-eyed as Rob removes his hand from her thigh, then sticks his finger into his mouth. "Nice bouquet– robust flavor. Tastes like someone who's enjoyed himself several times tonight." With a wink, Robin swaggers back from whence he came.

"And here I thought Devon was crazy." Exhausted, I slide from the bar to stand on shaky legs.

"You do realize Rob just ate your cum, right?" Grossed out, Bethany stares at me like I should be losing my shit instead of rolling with it.

Helping my wife stand, I wrap an arm around her waist, then lead her to the hallway, snatching her bag and jeans on our way by. "You do realize Devon's saliva was dried all over my dick, and I just fucked you with it. I also kissed you, after kissing him and sucking his cum off my hand and his junk... and I ate his ass. So let's not split hairs about grossness because Rob was curious to know what I tasted like. By law of seven-degrees of separation, we've all fucked each other by now."

"Dude! Your horizons just opened up this big." Beth parts her arms wide as we walk down the hallway. "HUGE! Little Rory Essex is growing up to be an adventurous bisexual machine. Way to go, husband!"

"You're so high." I rumble a chuckle, helping Beth up the stairs.

"So are you," she volleys back.

"Not as much as you."

"You sucked Devon's dick," she slurs, impressed.

Admitted without hesitation, "And I liked it."

CHAPTER TEN

The sound of video game gunfire filters out onto the front porch, so I let myself in. It wouldn't be the first time nobody heard me knocking, and it won't be the last, so I suspect that's the reason the Shithole's front door is never locked.

"Jesus, Ren!" Willow's husky voice hits my ears before I take one step into the house. "Who are these assholes you hooked up with online? I can't take any of them out."

"You're only as good as your competition." Hyper-focused on the game, Ren replies in a monotone voice as I shut the door behind me. "They're Toby's people."

"What the hell is Farmville's actual name? How is he so good? And why would a dude who's obsessed with Farmville play Halo? Unless he's an actual farmer?"

Snorting, I lean back against the door, watching Ren and Willow for a few minutes, knowing better than to walk between the coffee table and the ginormous TV. A few weeks back, I made the mistake of trying to sneak past, not wanting to disturb them. Before I made it to the kitchen, Willow was calling out to me, saying I murdered her game average because she was headshot while I blocked the TV.

Willow's an old-school gamer, whereas Ren shines at today's first-person shooters. It's hilarious to watch how serious Ren takes it, while Willow bitches and moans and calls everyone cheaters.

"Farmville's name is Roarke." Ren's eyes never leave the screen, which isn't a hard thing to do because the TV is at least seventy inches. Oh, to be nineteen again, with unlimited disposable income. "He's good because he has fifteen years' experience on us, and is almost old enough to be our dad."

"Probably been playing since gaming was invented… so why are we playing with him?" Willow whines, tossing her controller onto the sofa cushion as the respawn timer counts down. "I wanna have fun, not die every five seconds."

"Roarke's improving my game." Lips curling, Ren smirks as he takes out another player.

"Who's By-blow?" Willow picks up her controller and is dead within a second of respawning. "He's stalking all my respawn locations. Not cool, motherfucker. I wanna play Mario."

"Toby," Ren replies, but it sounds a helluva lot like *'you idiot'* when he says it. "I don't know what it means. I looked it up, and it confused the piss out of me. Toby's not a bastard."

"Toby's awesome– don't call him names. How that sweet kid can be so savage in the virtual world is beyond me." Willow shifts on the sofa, just staring at the screen, no longer playing. "I'm bowing out the next round. I'll read a comic book while you play from now on."

"Spanky, by-blow literally means a bastard, as in *illegitimate* kid." The game beeps down to its final seconds with Ren coming in third, with Farmville and By-blow in first and second, RevampyKitten came in last place without a single point– most definitely Willow. "Oh, hey!" Ren finally spots me.

"I knew better than to walk in front of the TV again," I murmur wryly, causing Willow to blush.

"I'm so embarrassed," Willow admits, gesturing to the TV. "I love gaming, but I totally suck at this game. I don't get it."

"Play the campaign," I offer up some much-needed advice. "Play the campaign on the easiest setting, working your way through all the difficulties. Once you beat it on Legendary, then you're ready for multiplayer against gamers like Roarke. They'll still annihilate you, but you'll hold your own. And, like Ren said, they'll teach you to be a better gamer."

Ren clicks his headphone on, drawing down the mic. "Roarke, I'll catch you in a few days. Gonna play the campaign with Willow." After a brief pause. "Yeah, I don't know why I didn't think of that earlier either. Tell Toby I'll text him later."

"So where are your roomies?" Leaning back against the door with a gift under my arm, I refuse to budge until I'm invited in.

"Essie's taking another nap." Willow worries her bottom lip, clutching a pillow to her chest. "That pregnancy business is for the birds. Sleep. Eat. Moan in pain. Sleep. Eat. Cry. I want no part of that hormonal stew." She winces in sympathy. "Can't wait to meet my nephew, though."

"Dev's holding down a lawn chair in the backyard." Ren's navigating the menu on the screen, setting up a co-op campaign on the easiest setting. "We keep checking on him through the kitchen window in between rounds, but it's pissing him off. Says he wants to be alone. The moody bastard from Devon's past has made a reappearance."

Taking that as my cue, "Enjoy this while it lasts," I warn the gamers. "They just announced the next Halo won't have split-screen capabilities." Chuckling, I leave Willow dumbfounded– as an old-school gamer, she's used to sharing a screen –and Ren cheering how he's going to start saving his pennies for another big-screen and system.

Stalking through the house like I own the place, I slip out the backdoor, to find Devon staring off into space. If it was anyone else, I'd stand still and watch his body language for a few minutes, but Devon has Ninja senses.

"Hey," Devon murmurs softly, not looking at me. "I'm not catatonic like I used to be, so don't freak out. I'm just thinking over my behavior."

"I thought–" hesitating, I choose my words wisely as I come to stand at Devon's shoulder. "I thought you forgave yourself for the past."

Devon's hand raises, seeking mine. Not even bothering to look around for nosy neighbors or roommates, I lean down to give him a kiss. I'm not going to hide it, and Devon doesn't seem like the skittish, embarrassed type. We haven't done anything sexual in the many weeks since the attic, just hanging out and getting to know each other, but we've been affectionate.

After a quick kiss, I slide into a seat, depositing the gift on the patio table as I do. "What's wrong?" No judgment or condemnation, my voice is filled with nothing but concern. Eyes flicking quickly across Devon's expression, I try to get a read on him.

"Today was a nine from start to finish," Devon admits to me, and I know he hasn't told another soul. Maybe his therapist, but he'd never worry Essie and his family. I remain quiet, knowing

Devon needs a listening ear, not someone passing out unsolicited advice on a subject they could never comprehend.

"Just one of those days– meds be damned, I was depressed. My past was battering inside my psyche, cravings were wreaking havoc on my system, my tics were overpowering, and temptation presented itself."

Leaning forward, Devon snatches a bottle of water off the table, then drains it in one large swallow. "All day, I was focused on the fact that I couldn't even have a goddamn Coke– the drink, not the blow," Devon mutters wryly, showing his dark sense of humor. "Did you know stimulants are hidden every-fucking-where?"

Dropping my hand into Devon's lap, I give him access to my wedding band. When Devon gets upset, he likes to fiddle with things. He only wore his wedding band for two weeks because it was distracting him. Fingertips rubbing against the cool metal, Devon spins the band around my finger. He's been contemplating a ring tattoo, but he's scared he'd scratch his skin off if his tics got bad. We're going to try a tattoo in a less accessible place first.

"It was a solid nine all day, no matter what. Then I had a traffic stop with Kyle. The guy had a warrant out for his arrest– failure to appear. Since I'm on restricted duty, Kyle trained his weapon on the guy while I searched him outside of his car. He had a baggie of crystal meth in his front pocket."

"Oh, Christ." Warring with myself, I don't pull Devon into a hug, knowing he needs to talk more than be comforted. He gets enough smothering from his family as it is, without me adding to it.

"That was as close to a ten as an addict could get." Devon shifts in his seat, acting as if his skin hurts. "I'd love to say I was strong enough, but it was Kyle who took it out of my hand. Because I was staring down at it, acting exactly as I am– a junkie."

"If you had taken it–"

"And survived," Devon interrupts me. "Good chance I would've overdosed if I used the amount I was used to when my tolerance was up. My body has reset."

Ignoring the interruption, "If you had taken it, it wouldn't have made you a bad person, or weak, or out of control. You would have used, and we would have gone from there."

"I still would've felt all those things, ya know?" Devon admits. "Because I'm feeling them now, and all I did was hold the baggie while in the commission of my duty."

"So you're sitting out here feeling down on yourself instead of feeling proud for winning a hard-fought battle in the war?"

"Not exactly." Devon's eyes cut in my direction, amusement riding his self-deprecation. "I lost it on Dad in the middle of the Batcave. Totally lost control, where I was shouting all our business for Dad's subordinates to hear. Every. Fucking. Horrific. Thing."

"Whoa…" spills silently, and I don't say anything else because I want Devon to get it out.

"I'm sure twenty years from now, it'll be hilarious. But Dad didn't care that I was blaming him for everything, because he was too terrified I was backsliding. He called Dr. Delaney in Arizona, and put the guy on speakerphone to listen to my tirade. When I calmed down and collapsed at Dad's desk, Dad talked to every single one of my doctors and therapists."

Silence descends, Devon's motionless with the exception of a single fingertip swirling my wedding band around my finger. After waiting about ten minutes as Devon stares off into space, dwelling deep inside his mind, I can't take it anymore.

"What happened next?" I coax, curious to know how Devon ended up sitting out in his backyard alone.

"I wasn't left alone for a second, because Dad was terrified I'd either take drugs or off myself. He even followed me into the bathroom stall. Then he drove my ass to my therapist here in town, waiting for two hours in the car. He took me to the Pink Taco Hut, and forced me to eat a balanced meal Clover made me. When he dropped me off, he made sure Ren knew not to leave me alone. Dad wouldn't give me a hug, and it was the first time I wanted one from him– so I stole one, and he broke down crying… I told Ren if he didn't leave me alone, I'd murder him in his sleep, which leads me here to now."

All of Devon's doctors and therapists want him to talk it out, think it over, even Bethany is notorious for this. But I think it makes it worse, because Devon ends up overanalyzing shit until the perception of what happened changes, no longer seeing it as it happened in reality. That's not my approach, which is why Devon enjoys my company.

"I brought you this–" Plucking the wrapped box off the table, I drop it into Devon's lap. "But I think tonight is more of a speedway night."

Devon's as intoxicated by Bad Rory as I am with Bad Devon. We've visited Jake at least five times, test driving the dealership's high-performance machines at the speedway. I always pussy out near one-seventy, but Devon has no stopping point, taking the cars to almost two hundred. Unlike me, Devon judges it by the RPMs, not his fear.

"It's Saturday night," Devon reminds me. "They have a race. Watching cars go fast, when I'm not the one driving them, makes me jealous and antsy." Curiosity getting the better of him, Devon tears into the wrapping paper, revealing the board game. "Othello?"

"Yeah, it's a one-on-one game, where you have to really concentrate." Blushing, I feel silly giving Devon a gift. "I thought it would help you focus on anything but what's going on inside your mind."

"Thank you," Devon murmurs in a heartfelt tone, clutching the box to his chest. "We'll play it a few times a week– maybe I'll teach one of the idiots inside the house."

"Ha!" I snort, understanding Devon's resentment toward his family. He's all talk, though. Devon loves the hell out of his family, hating it when they smother him, but missing them the second they aren't.

The despondent expression on Devon's face twists my guts, so I just roll with it. "How about we grab Essie and head over to my place. Leave Ren and Willow to their game."

"*They're so loud*," Devon stresses, senses hypersensitive. "Even when they don't mean to be."

"Wanna watch a movie?" I coax, needing Devon's intoxicating aura to reappear. "The girls will love hanging out with us."

"It's a Saturday night," Devon reminds me again. "Rush's biggest night of the week."

Flashing a naughty smirk, "I'm going to be Bad Rory tonight and play hooky."

Devon's response is to move quickly, lips capturing mine. He's pulling away before I can even react. "Thanks." Standing fluidly– sitting, then standing, in the blink of an eye –Devon tugs me from my seat. "Come with me. I gotta change and fetch Essie, but I won't force you to watch Ren and Willow play Halo."

"The girl is a disaster." I chuckle underneath my breath as Devon fetches his game and the discarded wrapping paper.

"I made Willow cry last night." Devon snickers sinisterly. "She was so pissed I beat her on Halo, and I'd never played before."

Peeking into the living room, we watch as Willow studiously listens to Ren's instruction as they play the campaign. After we sneak up the steps, I can't help myself. "You know she's going to learn how to play and go balls to the wall savage on Ren's ass."

"Fuck, yeah." Devon grins at me. "Willow's a competitive little shit... *holy fuck!*"

As we enter Devon's bedroom, I walk right into his back. Being a head and a half taller, he doesn't block the view.

"Oh. My. God." Essie stammers in a panic, quickly closing her thighs, but not fast enough. The toy is flung into the open nightstand drawer, vibrating loudly against the pressed wood. "I'm going to go die now." She tries to cover her lady bits, tugging down her t-shirt, but her baby bump gets in the way. She settles for grabbing her discarded pants, holding them in front of her area.

"Sweet Jesus," Devon purrs, and I chance a glance in his direction, finding his pupils blown. "Don't go– it was a beautiful show."

"I'm going to go drown myself in the bathroom." Essie slips off the bed, stumbling halfway to the bathroom as she drags her pants up her legs. "Sorry about that, Rory." Blushing a brilliant shade of red, Essie's freaking out.

"My fault– I invaded *your* bedroom," I point out, blushing just as badly. But I'm not sure Essie heard me, because she shuts herself in their bathroom.

"You left your vibrator running!" Devon shouts, completely shameless in his teasing. Plucking the purple phallic-shaped toy from the drawer, Devon sniffs it. Eyes bugging out, I watch in wonder as he peels his trousers off, stands to the side, then compares the toy to his own junk.

"I'm bigger, but I don't vibrate," he mutters in all seriousness. With the flick of a single fingertip, the toy stops vibrating. Devon wipes it off on his discarded trousers, then places it back in the drawer. "Your boyfriend is all safe and sound now, hun! My bad!"

"You are a disturbing fucker." Gobsmacked, all I can do is watch as Devon strips down completely naked then only pulls on a pair of thin sweats and a wife-beater. "You knew, didn't you?"

"Of course I did." Lips curled into a dirty smirk, Devon slips into a pair of flip-flops. "No woman naps that much– she won't let me go down on her anymore, saying I'm not getting anything from it. Pisses me off something fierce."

"What are you going to do?" Leaning against the door, I watch Devon stow Othello on top of his dresser, pitch the paper in the trash, and then fetch his wallet, keys, and cellphone.

"I'm going to hide Essie's vibrator, and every time she says she's going to go take a nap, I'm gonna sneak in here and eat the fuck outta that pussy." Devon eyes the drawer, looking like a man betrayed by his woman. "I'll do a better job than that piece of plastic."

"You get why she's doing it though, don't you?" I try to be the voice of reason.

"Yeah, that's what's pissing me the hell off." Stalking over to the bathroom door, Devon knocks lightly. "Hun, we're going over to their house to watch a movie– be sure to warn Beth, since I know you're on the phone with her right now."

Snorting, I try again. "Why don't you talk to her about it?"

"Don't you think I've tried?" Devon twists up his face, sneering. "We got into a huge fight last night, one Willow and Ren heard. Ren jumped in, telling Essie to stop stressing me out, which got me fighting with Ren. What a clusterfuck."

"Probably why today was a nine from the time you woke up," I mutter wryly. "You're supposed to avoid stress, remember?"

"Essie's so dang insecure, and the hormones are making her horny as fuck… and I can sense it, so being denied really rubs me wrong."

"I can hear you, you know?" Essie grumbles, stepping out of the bathroom, face still bright red.

Walking by me to intercept his wife, Devon grabs my crotch. "Essie, Rory got insta-hard the second he saw you rubbing one out." Fingers clench to the point of pain, bringing me back to full mast. "Take a guy at his word, okay? If you don't want me going down on you, say so. But it better not be for some idiotic selfless reason, like you think I'm not getting anything out of it."

"Save me," Essie pleads, looking like she wants to put a paper bag over her head and hide, but I'm the guy getting groped by her husband. "I'm fat–"

"You're pregnant," Devon and I say in unison.

"And uncomfortable," Essie continues. "We don't need to mess around."

"And horny," Devon stresses. "I wanna mess around, hard-on or not. Okay?"

"Okay," Essie whispers, completely mortified.

"That better not be an okay where you just agree to shut me up," Devon calls Essie out on her shit. "It better be an okay, where you understand what I'm saying."

I need to have a private conversation with Essie, because she's never going to believe Devon, thinking he's trying to save her hurt feelings. The woman has it in her head that an erection is the only indicator of a man wanting her. She's not going to believe Beth because my wife doesn't have a dick.

"Essie, you and I are going to have a talk," I warn. "But not right now," because she won't be receptive to it with how embarrassed she is. "Later. We're just going to go hang out after a stressful week. Sound good?"

"Yeah." Essie squeezes my arm in thanks, then stalks over to her dresser to collect her purse. Erupting into a giggle fit, "Wish you guys would've waited another minute before invading the bedroom. I was about to come. Now I'm gonna be frustrated on top of the humiliation."

CHAPTER ELEVEN

"Why the hell did we let the girls pick the movie?" Devon stretches, yawning dramatically. "I'm so goddamn bored."

The four of us are smushed on the sofa, Devon and I are side-by-side with our wives practically sitting in our laps. The girls are glued to the screen, enraptured by a sappy Nicholas Sparks movie. I've been pretending to watch it, eyeing the stack of my DVDs that always goes unwatched.

"You said you felt emasculated before." Devon elbows me in the ribs. "If another character kicks it, loses their job, gets abused, suffers from dementia, or falls off a bull, I'm gonna do a shot."

"You can't drink," I murmur out the side of my mouth in Devon's direction. "But if you could, I'd join ya. Just hoping the bull goes on a rampage–"

"And brings friends." Devon cackles to entertain himself.

"Running of the bulls, Nicholas Sparks style."

"Shhh…" Beth hisses, annoyed. "The good part's coming up."

"There's a good part?" Devon mutters, earning a palm slapped over his mouth. "When is the dry part going to end?"

"Have you seen The Lucky One?"

"Of course," Devon growls from beneath Essie's palm. "Hormonal pregnant wife, remember? These DVDs have been playing nonstop."

"There's a sex scene in The Lucky One. Zac Efron looked pretty hot."

"Not gonna go there with ya, bud," Devon taunts me as the girls giggle. "I don't shop around for guys– ain't wired that way." Devon doesn't mean in the straight, gay, bi way.

After a heavy conversation, Devon explained he needs to be connected to someone to want to have sex with them. He admitted it took until he started hanging around me to come to terms with being demisexual. He didn't even know what the term meant until recently. He finds all sorts of people attractive, appreciates their appearance, but that doesn't translate into lust. Lust grows from friendship or romance only. Doesn't have to be love, but it has to be real intimacy.

"Maybe we'll watch that one next," Beth whispers against my neck. "I'll ogle hot guys with you anytime. Efron's ass is *tight*."

A shudder rolls down my spine, alerting everyone on the sofa that I'm down for that plan.

"I'm bored," Devon grumbles again, voice sounding bitchy. "Need fun." Beth's plucked out of my lap and tossed on Devon's vacated cushion, with Essie rolling into her side.

"Holy shit, you move fucking fast, you goddamn Ninja," Beth complains, sounding gobsmacked. "How the hell are you so strong?"

"I work out." Devon drops to his knees. "Bored as fuck– need fun." Hands land on my thighs. "You girls can watch us or the movie– your choice."

To the background soundtrack of a woman weeping uncontrollably on the screen and the girls muttering *ohmygod... ohmygod... ohmygod... ohmygod* on repeat, I stare down at the guy who feels powerful on his knees.

"It's either déjà vu or PTSD flashbacks, but I swear I've heard Bethany chant that same phrase before," Devon mutters wryly, causing Beth to lose her shit. Head jacking backward, Bethany laughs so hard and loud she causes all of us to join her.

"You're jealous," I taunt, raising my eyebrow. "Admit it. You're jealous of a movie star?"

"You think I'm going to deny it?" Devon reaches for my fly. "First of all, start wearing sweats around the house. Second of all, you are not allowed to have any friends who aren't related to one of us, or married to one of us."

"Third of all..." Beth snorts, twisting to get a better view. "This reminds me of the old Devon. Possessive. Controlling. Demanding."

"Still the same Devon, Beth." Rolling his eyes, Devon smirks up at me. "Seriously, invest in some pants made of Jersey cotton. I can't do denim anymore." With a struggle, multiple hands help me out of my pants, leaving my boxers behind because they won't mess with Devon's tactile issues. "If you haven't figured it out yet, I'm possessive of everyone on this couch– that's it."

"Fair enough." Swallowing thickly, I can't believe what I'm seeing. Devon leans in slowly, mouth opening, tongue peeking out, then he bites my thigh. Hard. "Fuck me!" I shout, nerves confused by the conflicting messages my brain is sending.

"That can be arranged," Devon purrs against my thigh, fluttering the hairs to tickle me.

"Oh…" Essie leans around Beth, mouth gaping open with her pupils blown. "Turn the TV off, Beth. Nothing will ever top this."

Refusing to be ignored, Devon moves fast, body rolling up mine until we're face-to-face. Surprise has my mouth already open, allowing an invading tongue to enter. Moaning, I drag Devon into my lap, knees straddling my hips.

Writhing against each other, we kiss with our wives watching on, and I feel no shame or guilt, or judgment or hurt from the girls. Since Devon only has one shot, he's changed from getting off quickly as a teenager, to enjoying kissing and grinding against each other for a long time. Our *hug* yesterday lasted Devon's entire lunch break and then some.

"I'm wearing sweats from now on," rolls off my tongue like a moan. Moving my hands from gripping Devon's hips to sliding beneath the soft fabric of his pants, I cup his ass, biting my fingertips in until the flesh dimples.

Moaning loudly, Devon begins sucking on my throat while rolling his bulge against my belly. We experience an intense make-out session with the girls chanting *ohmygod… isthisreallyhappening… didIjustcomeinmypanties… ohmygod…*

Pulling away, panting, "I'm gonna suck your dick," Devon threatens, face flushed with lust. "I'm gonna drink your cum down my throat."

Holyshit… thisreallyishappening… ohmygod…

"Yeah." Swallowing thickly, it takes several tries to speak. "I'm more than fine with that."

"Then." Devon issues a dramatic pause, turning his face to glance at the girls to include them in the festivities. "Since your refractory period is like three minutes– and I'd be fucking jealous of that if it wasn't for the fact that I get to use it to my advantage –you girls are going to ride our dicks."

"I'm good with that," I repeat.

"Uh-huh… yeah… so down," Beth stammers.

"*Holyshitisthisreallyhappening*," Essie strings into a singular word, voice slurred with lust.

"But first." Another dramatic pause, because Devon's bloated with power. "We're going to get something through my wife's thick skull." Dark eyes flick in Essie's direction. "If you're not horny, say no. But if you're saying it out of some misguided selflessness, knock it off. I get one ejaculation a day, and I'm thankful I do, because most men who take the same mood stabilizer cocktail as I do don't."

Devon looks at all three of us in turn, starting and ending with Essie, making sure she's listening.

"So I like waking my wife up with a breakfast of happy pussy, and my soft cock doesn't get a vote. It makes me feel manly, and powerful, and I start the day in a great mood. I regain my ability to get hard by mid-morning. So when I get home, I want another feast to unwind and de-stress. Even though I'm harder than a rock, I don't want to get off yet. I like the pressure, the tension, the feeling of control I have over my own body. I'm saving it for later. Then, when we go to bed, I love giving and getting a massage, and falling asleep after making love. None of that has anything to do with my dick, and everything about connecting with you, Essie."

With tears glittering in her eyes, Essie nods quickly. "Okay."

"Okay, I'm just agreeing with you?" Holding his wife's gaze, Devon doesn't even blink. "Or, okay, I finally understand?"

"Okay, I understand." Chuckling at herself, Essie blushes. "And I'm horny nonstop thanks to the hormones, so I'm not going to say no unless I'm feeling like shit."

"Just so we're clear–" Devon is riding high on a power-trip. "I'm going to suck Rory's cock now. If anyone isn't okay with that, speak now, or forever hold your peace… and I mean, *forever*. No bringing it back up in a fight. No using it against me.

No using it for an agenda to validate an insecurity. This is a forever thing. Non-negotiable. I'm gonna be sucking Rory's dick for life."

The girls share a look, and I don't bother looking at Beth, because I know her response. I let Beth deal with Essie. "Forever has a nice ring to it– guaranteed blowjobs for life, I'm down with that."

Laughing that goddamn addictive, intoxicating sinful laugh, Devon leans forward to bite my bottom lip. Glowing like the sun, Devon's radiating an energy only he releases.

"I want you to suck Rory's dick," Essie stammers, blushing yet brave enough to admit what she wants. For a woman as gorgeous as she is, Essie's surprisingly innocent. "I really want to watch… unless it's too private," she adds, blushing brighter.

"Watch?" Beth's the braver, experienced one. "We're going to help."

"Holy hell!" Arching my back, writhing, it takes Devon grabbing my junk to keep me from popping.

"You totally suck as an edging mentor," Devon murmurs wryly. "It's a good thing you'll be ready to go again so quickly." Scooting down my body, the girls get out of Devon's way. "Gonna suck the cum outta your thick dick now, make you forget all about Zac Efron's tight ass." Fingers tug my boxers out of the way. "My ass is tighter, I bet."

"Is that on the table?" It's my turn to stammer.

"Yeah," Devon breathes against my belly. "Yours too."

I'm far from innocent, not after the education I received from the deviant trio. But they knew me well, which is why they never invited me into the Playroom. I had sex in front of my friends when I was in high school, but never again after I graduated. I peeked into the Playroom out of curiosity, never finding it anything I wanted to do.

I know I shocked Auggie with the lengths I was willing to go to win Beth's freedom from their arrangement, never planning on actually attending a Playroom function.

Aside from Rob watching me fuck Beth on the bar, I've been damn near innocent, never once bridging the gap to ménage. Fooling around with Devon feels natural, but this feels downright naughty, but in a good way.

"I wanna be Bad Rory," I purr, fingers seeking Devon's hair, knowing he gets off on us being rougher with each other when it comes to sex. "Suck my dick like you mean it– show our wives how it's done."

Unable to keep my eyes open, I lean back, cradling my head against the cushions. A silent moan escapes my throat as a hot mouth envelops my cock, damn near deep-throating me on the first suck. Palms cupped around Devon's skull, my arms go up and down with his rhythmic movements.

The feel of Devon's moans reverberating against my flesh, adds to the heightened sensation. Tiny mouths pepper my thighs with kisses, startling me. A juxtaposition to the girls' gentleness, Devon nips my sack with his front teeth, causing me to jump.

Laughing sadistically, Devon uses my freak out to his advantage, spreading my thighs wider. Not sure what to do with myself, I reach over to touch both of the girls, resting my palms on their heads. Not pushing, I thread my fingers into their hair, tickling at their scalps.

A sharp bark of a laugh is torn from my throat as Bethany's mouth encloses around me, sucking harder than she usually does, like it's a competition to see who can suck the cum out of my balls. Keeping my eyes closed, I get off on the sensory deprivation enlivening my other senses. It's also a real trip to figure out who's doing what to me.

Mouths change. "Jesus fuck!" I shout in a panic, tugging Essie's hair until my cock pops out of her mouth. "Edging ain't gonna work tonight, girl. You got one helluva mouth on you." Huffing in pants, "Gimme thirty seconds, and get back on my dick."

Essie's laughter is embarrassed, but I'm surprised to hear how proud Beth and Devon sound of their girl. "Yeah… yeah, just like that." Groaning, head hitching backward, my hips lift off the cushion, thrusting slightly into Essie's mouth. Scorching hot and wet, the suction and depth is unexpected, drawing my sack up tight to my body. "Gonna come!" I warn, seconds away.

"Mine," Devon snarls, acting possessive, and it's the funniest fucking thing to watch the three of them fight over my cock. Laughing, cum spurts out every time my belly contracts.

I'm so distracted, I don't get to enjoy my orgasm, but it's the most entertaining thirty seconds of my existence.

The girls are giggling, piling on top of Devon, not truly wanting to suck my dick, but finding it funny as all hell to piss Devon off.

"Not cool," Devon pouts, coming in to lick me from my taint, across my sack, up my dick, all the way to my belly button.

"Get over here," I purr, tugging Devon up onto the cushion next to me. Palming the nape of his neck, I give him a kiss worthy of a Nicholas Sparks movie, causing him to writhe around on the sofa. I pull away before he's ready, because he was getting too into it.

Expression soft, I gaze into Devon's eyes, showing every emotion playing out in my mind. "Did you come?" I ask, knowing Devon gets so deep into making out, he sometimes has to grab his junk to stop from coming.

"Almost." Blushing, Devon flashes me his coy look, where he gazes at me through his lashes with those intense dark eyes. It took me a while, but I know it's on purpose, not at all innocent, and completely his way of trying to seduce me.

The coy look belongs solely to me, just as I've seen Devon employ other seduction tactics on Essie, even on Beth. Most of the time, I'm not sure he even realizes he's doing it, but he does have the ability to pull it out on demand.

"No wonder you're terrified of Essie sucking you off, even just for a little bit," I tease, eyes flicking to the woman. "A little foreplay would be game-over." Turning to Beth, "Did you know your bestie was a masterful cocksucktress?"

Releasing a sinful giggle, Beth slides into my lap, straddling my hips. "Oh, Essie's had a lot of practice, but she didn't enjoy it as much as she did tonight." Wiggling on my lap, I gasp in shock as Beth's damp cunny lips side all over my dick.

"Well, that's something else," I murmur drowsily, eyes cutting to the side to witness Essie doing the same to Devon. The only difference is that Devon is cocked and at the ready, totally lost in lust. Hands and mouth touching all he can reach on his wife. Essie's satisfied moans are music to my ears.

"May I?" I ask politely, gesturing where they're rubbing against one another. Devon leans back into the cushions and

Essie leans back on his thighs in invitation. Reaching over, I grab Devon's cock, giving a few pumps because I can't help myself.

Steadying Essie with a hand on her hip, I help her slide down Devon's shaft. "As soon as you feel Devon's dick start to throb, stop moving– no kissing, no caressing." Intrigued, my eyes flick back and forth, taking in both Essie's and Devon's expressions as they join as one. "Wait about thirty seconds, then start riding him again. If you flex your hips enough, you can rub your clit on the base of his dick. Here–"

With both hands, I position Essie over Devon, then slip one hand between them to make sure they're lined up right. Essie jumps as my fingertip caresses her clit, so I decide to do it for a few extra seconds to light her on fire. She's so turned on, I'm able to roll her clit between my forefinger and thumb, tugging slightly.

Devon's doing what I'm doing, eyes flicking back and forth to read our expressions, when I thought he'd be angry or possessive. "My cock's already spazzing out," he admits breathlessly. "If I make it three minutes, it's gonna be a miracle."

"I know you guys haven't had much sex." Understatement that. They've probably had sex less than fifteen times in their lives– maybe even combined. "Just showing you a way that Essie will get hers, and you can control your orgasm a bit. The thrusts will be shallower, which is a plus for you, Devon. Lots of clit-action, which is good for you, Ess. Okay."

Pulling away, I find my wife gazing at me with love and adoration, and a helluva lot of pride. "You're good with them," she purrs, running her palms up and down my chest while she rubs her pussy along my flaccid cock.

In a way, I'm glad I already got off, because I'm able to empathize with Devon. Instead of being hyper-focused on getting off, I concentrate on touching my wife while enjoying touches that I'd normally be too impatient to appreciate.

Kissing and sucking at each other's flesh, hands rub wherever they can reach. Beth moaning into my ear has blood rushing south, but not enough to get me fully hard, not so soon. Drugged, eyes droopy, the sensation of Beth's skin sliding against mine is an intimacy I'd usually take for granted, more worried about the finale.

Devon snags my wrist, tugging my hand back to where he's joined with Essie. He flips my hand over, palm up, then his hand disappears. Parting my fingers in a V-shape, Devon's cock slides back and forth between them. Essie's clit rubs on my palm in a press and release motion as she rides his cock, leaving dampness behind.

Beth and I grunt in unison as Devon's hand presses between our bodies, giving my cock a few healthy jerks to get more blood flowing. "Curl your fingers around my cock and slip them inside Essie," he breathes into my ear, causing me to shudder and grow rock hard. "Do it. Finger-fuck my wife."

Obeying, because that's what I always do when Devon whispers sinful demands in my ear, I nearly come at the feel of Essie's body sucking at my fingers while Devon's cock caresses us both.

"Bad Rory is a filthy fucker." Devon moans against the side of my throat, then he licks me. "Gonna finger-fuck your wife– let your cock rest for a minute while I do it."

"Holy shit!" Bethany gasps in surprise, falling forward until her breasts are pressed against my face. "Yeah, hard."

Chuckling evilly, Devon's fingers are moving rapidly inside my wife, causing her to have to clutch the back of the sofa or fall off my lap.

Our personalities are obvious right now. Essie's moving slowly, moaning breathily at the same speed I'm thrusting my fingers in and out of her, while I fight for space with Devon's cock. Beth and Devon are on another level altogether. Devon's violently finger-fucking Beth, her pussy is making squishy sounds, with his wrist pounding against my pelvis hard enough to bruise.

"Yes!" Beth arches her back, head thrown back, hair trailing down in a cascade, as she rides Devon's fingers. I've seen the same intensity between us on countless occasions, but she never looked this uninhibited when I'd sneak into the Playroom to watch her.

It's not because it's Devon, or because it's me, or because Essie's with us. It's the trust. It's the safety. Trust and safety make all the difference.

Monogamy and fidelity are most definitely not synonymous for us. This is as fun as it is emotional and pleasurable, but I feel closer to Beth because we're sharing in the experience.

Noticing the changes in my wife, I know she's on the verge of falling off the edge. Devon yanks his hand out of Beth, splattering me with the rain she's releasing. My cock is gripped in a masculine fist, then shoved inside Beth's clenching pussy.

"They wouldn't let me get you off," Devon pants against my neck, tone possessive. "So I just abused Beth's pussy." Laughing evilly, "Didn't realize she'd get off on the punishment."

"Not. Cool." Gasping, there's no way I'm going to be able to ride out Beth's orgasm, not with how hard she's riding me and with her pussy strangling my cock. "Gonna come!"

Slipping my fingers from Essie, I roll her clit between my fingers, wanting her to go with me. Devon's silent laughter vibrates against my side. "Who's the master of edging now?" Then he lets go too, proving he's picked up some timing skills over the past few weeks.

"Seriously!" I gesture at the screen, totally outraged. "Those cars do not handle like that. A SWAT truck versus a Civic? *Pfft...*" Blowing a raspberry, I glare at the screen. "Car chases are fun and all, but do some research first."

"Sex scene is always next," Devon deadpans from next to me on the sofa. "I could buy a Civic taking out a SWAT truck before I'd buy our half dead hero getting some before getting the bullet out of his shoulder."

Devon and I broke into my DVD stash while the girls are more interested in watching us interact. After playtime was over, we took turns taking showers while Beth and I made snacks. Now the girls are lying on our bed, with their feet at the headboard. Beth's on her belly, watching me instead of the tablet Essie's tapping on. They're noshing on Beth's secret, emergency stash of chocolate she doesn't think I know exists.

Essie's drowsy, but Beth's on high-alert, watching Devon and me like specimens in an experiment. I can't block her out, and I have no idea how Devon is, because that guy can feel a fly buzzing in the air across the loft. He had a hissy fit because a stray hair landed on his arm earlier.

Exaggerated moaning has Devon and me busting a gut. "Told ya!" Devon calls, elbowing me in the ribs. "Without fail."

Tilting my head to the side, my eyes widen as the hero takes the heroine right there in the rubble of the latest site of a shootout. With blood, gore, and dead bodies littering the area, they're tearing off each other's clothing, not even being mindful of mortal wounds.

"Yeah, that ain't realistic– that guy needs to be in the OR immediately." Tilting my head farther to the side. "Sure is hot, though."

"You think that's hot?" Devon's now looking at me just like my wife is. Our eyes connect across the loft, and her lips curl into an amused smirk.

"You don't?" The beefy guy is pile-driving the skinny chick with huge tits into next week. Fingers are clawing flesh speckled with blood and covered in a dark, greasy substance from the explosions. Their clothing has tiny cuts from the shrapnel, showing off flashes of enticing flesh.

"Nah," Devon mutters with a shrug, body movements jarring me slightly. "I've been horny since puberty struck, so I can appreciate that the scene is hot, but it does nothing for me."

"Nothing?" Shocked, I gape at Devon instead of looking at the screen as the scene reaches the climax. "What about porn?"

"It's not like I can sit around and jerk off to it." Devon releases a self-deprecating laugh that has me wincing in sympathy. "I used to watch it when I was thirteen to get ideas and see how women tick. Even back then, when I'd be jerking it like ten times a day, I didn't do it to porn. I've watched it since for instruction, but nothing more."

"Huh?" I grunt, completely floored by how differently we tick. Not saying I'm normal and Devon's abnormal, but I have a hard time wrapping my mind around how Devon thinks. Porn and my junk has gotten me through some boring times. It's no wonder Beth's watching us like she's cataloging info for another case study.

"So you used to jerk off nonstop, but nothing in the past seven years?" I want to tread lightly, but it would only piss Devon off, thinking I'm pitying him.

Face twisting with anger, Devon's dark eyes zero in on me. "I was what I was, even back then. Do you have any idea the bullshit I hear all the time?"

"Tell me." I notice Essie's head pop up– we already had Beth as our captive audience. No doubt an open Devon is a rarity. He's more likely to write it down, then pass the journal to Essie. Hearing it in his voice is no doubt a new experience. I've never caught sight of that journal. All interactions we have are vocal or physical.

"People gossip, right?" Devon turns on the sofa to face me, smaller body easily folding cross-legged. "They mean well, but it rubs me raw. *It's not your fault. You shouldn't be guilty– ashamed. Did you hear Devon has sexual issues? Must be being raped did that to him. You only like sucking cock because you're reliving a traumatic experience. Poor Devon, being assaulted changed his sexual orientation.* All bullshit."

When Devon gets defensive and angry, he doesn't look away like most people do. Glaring me down in challenge, the guy makes me feel an inch big.

"I know it's *not* my fault, goddamn it. Telling me that over and over again is like the well-meaning person is giving me *permission* to feel as I already fucking do, like they have ownership over my damn emotions. I'm *not* ashamed– I don't feel guilty. They have no right to bring up what happened to me, when it's the most private experience of someone's existence. It's a power-trip, not well-meaning advice from assholes who have never experienced it, and hopefully never will. It's not for public consumption."

Torn between comforting Devon and allowing him to let it out, I freeze when all I want to do is hug the poor bastard. But I know that will be seen as pity, and I'll get cold-cocked instead of hugged back.

"My therapists in the past, they told me not to feel ashamed because my body betrayed me. *I don't.* I don't need permission to feel what I already feel, then wonder if it's their passive-aggressive way of telling me I *should* feel ashamed. My body did what it was programmed to do. I'm glad it did what it was supposed to do."

"What do you mean?" I try to empathize with Devon, but it's impossible since no one's brain on the planet functions on his wavelength.

"Even back then, I only wanted Essie because she was Essie. I was horny as fuck, but that didn't mean I was trolling for pussy at the high school. I didn't give a fuck about getting any from anyone else. Yeah, I'd love to blame the impotency on PTSD and traumatic amnesia. But anyone who has ever done hardcore drugs or is a raging alcoholic, they will tell you pumping toxic chemicals into your bloodstream makes it impossible to get hard. You don't want it anyway– you want your vices. I didn't have Essie, was fucked in the head, and mainlining enough drugs to knock out an elephant. I didn't give a shit about jerking off to porn, and it had nothing to do with what happened to me."

"After rehab–"

"A few weeks after I was out of detox, I started getting hard again like I did when I was young. But I still didn't care about getting off. It was a power-trip for me. The fact that Essie's pregnant is a testament that our baby was meant to exist. Now, I could probably knock her up a billion times over. Back then, it was a goddamn miracle. The uppers helped connect my mind and body enough to do it a few times."

"So it's not Alejandro who haunts your dreams?" Bethany projects across the loft, voice quiet and respectful.

"Of course he does," Devon spits. "I don't feel shame– I feel *rage*." He fists his chest, glaring at someone only he can see. "Rage that I'm terrified. Rage that I'll always *feel* terrified. Rage that I had no control over what happened to my body. Rage that people dehumanize others. But I'm conflicted by how Alejandro treated me."

Watching Devon go from anger, to fear, to gutted has me reaching over to hold his hand. "What do you mean?" Devon never talks to me about this, finding freedom in escaping his past while we hang out.

"Alejandro made me give him a blowjob while I jerked off, and that has nothing to do with why I enjoy giving blowjobs. It wasn't about what was happening, but the complete and total fucking head-trip. Afterward, he tormented Ren and me, to the point I asked him to fuck me to save Ren. A billion hours of therapy has me seeing it in a different light. I'd felt ashamed that I caved– that I was brave yet stupid enough to sacrifice myself to save my brother, when Alejandro never planned to touch Ren. So I doubt myself, thinking if I'd just held out, Dad would've arrived and I never would've been raped. Alejandro had me believing it was consensual, because I begged him to do it, and got off while it happened."

"Gaslighting?" I blurt out, remembering Devon said his attacker had done that to him. "Flipped it around until you thought you were at fault. Twisted with your head until you doubted yourself and did what they always planned for you to do, but made you think it was your idea."

"Yeah, Alejandro twisted with my head so bad, he even had me apologizing that I was too small because he got off too quickly." Devon barks a bitter laugh, sounding sickened with himself. Getting a faraway look on his face, *I would've lasted longer, but you're too tight. I'm sorry, Ale.* I felt bad his ego was bruised."

"Devon." Bethany's whisper is louder than a gunshot. Devon and I both look up to find Beth and Essie holding one another while crying.

"Doesn't matter," Devon mumbles sheepishly. "So when I hear the gossip, how my sexuality is fucked because of what happened to me, it makes me so fucking angry. *I'm me.* I would've wanted to mess around with guys as long as I connected to one like I did with Essie. The blowjob with Kurt– it was only a test, and I passed. It had nothing to do with Alejandro. But the sick thing is, I feel grateful to him for not hurting me, for showing me it would feel good… for making my body do what it was supposed to do."

Devon flows to his knees, kneeling on the sofa cushion, making sure he can see all three of us at once. "Here's the head-trip, the thing people will never understand. Like how the abuse between a mother and son doesn't exist inside a vacuum. Neither one of us would've existed, the victim and victimizer, if someone had stepped in and stopped one of us from giving or taking. It's not Stockholm syndrome, but it's always going to be riding me.

With Alejandro, a big part of me wants to thank him for not hurting me, for not taking one more thing away from me... the ability to enjoy sex, even as I'm fighting being demisexual, my mental illness, and my mood stabilizer cocktail. He showed me what my body was meant for, and that's the head-trip."

Watching Devon struggle to rein in his emotions does indescribable things to me– I hurt me for him. But it also makes me feel proud of him, and proud that he chose me to be in his life.

Our friendship is built on different things than his friendship with Beth and his partnership with Essie. I don't let Devon dwell in the past. I don't let him overanalyze until it breathes new life into the events he's already escaped and survived.

Insight is one thing– backsliding is an entirely different beast.

Lunging as quickly as possible, since Devon truly is a Ninja, I grab the guy and fling him over my shoulder. "What the–" he doesn't struggle because he's too stunned by the attack.

"Gonna give you a good night's sleep for once," I vow, getting choked up. Safety should be a guarantee, not a reward. We all take it for granted until we meet a survivor. "Part like the Red Sea, ladies," I warn a split-second before I dump Devon on our bed.

Beth grabs for the chocolate– *priorities* –and Essie snatches up the Kindle Fire. They stow their treasures in the nightstand drawers, then sit on opposite edges of the mattress, with Devon lying in the center near the foot of the bed.

Confused, Devon stares up at me, vulnerability wafting from his pores. "Tonight, you don't have to sleep with your back on the mattress to protect yourself, never truly sleeping because you're watching the door. And you're not going to panic as you spoon Essie because your back is exposed.

Tears shine up at me, and I sense Devon's not the only one too choked up to speak. "Let's pull back the blankets and call it a night." Being the one ordering three people around is new for me, especially when Devon is around. But he must really want it, because he obeys without a second's hesitation.

After some maneuvering, Devon and I are back-to-back in the center of the mattress, spooning our wives. The blankets fall over us, shutting the world out. Devon shudders, scooting closer to me, hot flesh searing into mine. "I feel so safe," is breathed so softly I strain to hear it, and even then I doubt it was ever spoken.

Beth rolls over to face me, like we usually sleep. In the darkness, a little light filters in from the pole lights illuminating the parking lot. My wife finally releases the emotions she's been holding back from me. Crying, sobbing silently, Beth's relief steals my breath.

In this moment, I realize the gravity of our situation. Everyone was keeping the truth from me, while they lived in a constant state of terror and grief. Beth didn't push me toward Devon for any reasons dealing with me.

Devon needed someone who wasn't freaking out around him, watching him like a hawk– he needed someone who treated him like he was anyone else.

Since I didn't realize Devon was in any danger, our interactions were pure. Beth would do anything for her best friends, even sharing her husband, to ensure Devon survived the next seventy years' worth of days filled with strict schedules and endless temptation.

"Devon's gonna be okay," I whisper to my wife, the rightness of the statement ringing in my tone. "I promise."

CHAPTER TWELVE

Managing a club has its advantages. Dancing, I know exactly how to move my body to the beat and not look like a dang fool while doing it. Another advantage is that I have complete and total run of the place. Rush is hopping with more people than we usually get on a Saturday night in the middle of February after Uncle Sam passes out tax refunds. When I want to host a private party, I slap a notice on the front doors, and do whatever I want inside Rush.

A requirement is being a social butterfly, and I feel no shame in that anymore. Bethany is a social creature to an extent, always relieved we live in Rush so she can sneak off and get a minute to herself. Except tonight is all about us– months after our wild wedding in Vegas, we're finally celebrating with our friends and family.

On the hottest night in August, Rush's air conditioning can't keep up with the bodies packed on the dance floor. Sweating and panting, I dance within a circle of bodies suggestively rubbing up against me, with my wife in my arms, showing off her bump and grind.

"Must get a drink," I rasp out, mouth drier than the Sierra. "No, stay." I pry Bethany's hands off my hips, then slap them on the nearest dancer. Drunk and giggling, Beth jumps on Ren's back, grabbing for Willow's hands.

"Hey, girlfriend!" Beth slurs over the sound of the music. "Ren can support us– c'mon and crawl up here with me. The view is incredible… can see everybody."

Shaking my head while laughing, I leave poor Ren to defend himself as Beth and Willow use him as a stepladder. He loves everything female, so the guy is in heaven as he hops to the beat with Beth and Willow clinging to his neck.

I catch sight of Devon and Essie sort of slow dancing in the distance. Their hands are joined, and they're tugging the other's arms like they're little kids, swaying back and forth in a jerky motion. Too cute, especially since Essie's belly is starting to get really big. Except Devon's wearing that fake as shit smile he gets when he's uncomfortable. Looking beyond the couple, I notice they're completely surrounded by Devon's brothers in blue and their dates, which is the cause of the pained smile. Devon loathes being babysat and stifled. People need to trust him, because Devon needs to prove he can trust himself.

"Congratulations!" a gaggle of Malcolm and Clover's spawn sing as I swagger by. I stop for a few minutes to dance with them, showing Seth a few killer moves. The kid's a quick study, but Weston's not. Poor guy reminds me of a newborn giraffe. I assure the boy it's just a phase I survived, eventually his feet will communicate with his brain– six and a half feet is a long span for a developing mind. Not that Weston pays much attention, because Opal's son shows me a few moves of his own.

"I'll be taking that with me," I croon to Violet, removing the drink she was hiding for Seth in the folds of her skirt. In one large gulp, I swallow down the rum and Coke, then pass the empty glass back to the disappointed girl. "Sorries, not losing my liquor license for your rite of passage. Go get drunk in a field out in the middle of nowhere like I had to."

Dancing away, I can't make it two feet without a hug, kiss, or a chat. It's a good twenty minutes before I pop out by the bar, tongue wagging for a drink. Walking around the bar like I own the place, I start mixing my own drink while checking out the tableau before me.

Auggie's closed himself off to a lot of people in the past few weeks, refusing to talk about what's bothering him. Bethany arranged for an intervention, tonight of all nights, since he couldn't *not* come. She invited all the intervention members because Auggie wouldn't think twice about that, unless he looked too closely.

Auggie's sitting at the bar, Isis on one side of him and Robin on the other. On the bartender's side, Auggie's entire family stands solemnly. From his sister to his grandparents.

Giving them some respect, I ignore what's going on while I make up a few drinks because Carrie's being run ragged. "Hey, neighbor!" I sing, plopping the drinks back onto the bar to free up my arms. I tug Tina into my arms, squeezing the beautiful girl. "Long time, no see– miss you rooming on the other side of me."

Laughing lightly, Tina squeezes me back, happy to know she's welcome around here, no matter what Auggie says. "It's good to be home, even for a few days. I missed the vibe of this place, sober or not."

"Good." Holding Tina at arm's length, I recognize the look of a person high on life instead of drugs. Her skin is flawless, glowing with good health, and her eyes are vibrant and clear of the taint. "You look amazing, girl."

"Hey," Tina pulls away, then tucks a smaller blond guy underneath her arm. "Do you remember my uncle, Tobias– Toby?"

"Toby?" Mouth gaping open, I haven't seen the guy since he was a little kid. Toby's the baby in the Kline family, so he was raised more as Tina and Auggie's baby brother instead of their uncle. "What have you been up to? Going to school somewhere?"

Blushing, the kid's adorable. Toby looks exactly like Tina, blue-eyed and blond-haired, except he's radiating innocence.

"I-I-I had to get away from it all," he stammers cryptically. "I moved to New York, and I'm going to school part-time there. Just visiting for Auggie." His eyes flick toward the distraught man. "I'm a symptom of what's wrong with him."

It's on the tip of my tongue to ask, but one look at Lisa and Patrick has all the tumblers clicking into place. Auggie's mom might be a pushover, but his grandfather is a pastor, and he's not backing down, and neither is his father. "I hope you have some fun while you're here, at least. Where are you staying?"

"We're at the Spook House," Tina fills in. A few weeks ago, Isis and Auggie moved home, leaving only Beth and me residing here. I'm close to renting out the other lofts to keep the deviant trio from ever attempting to move back.

"Well, that can't be too much fun," I murmur out the side of my mouth at Tina, causing her to giggle. At first I assume it's an echo, but then I realize Toby's laugh is identical to his niece's.

"Can I get anyone something to drink while I'm back here? 'Bout ready to hit the dance floor again."

"Do you have any scotch that's not on the shelf?" A guy steps forward, when I hadn't seen him lurking near the rear of the bar. He's a tiny fellow, with darker skin and tight ringlets. I do a double-take, mouth gaping. "Or perhaps something that induces calming effects?"

"Oh, hey… yeah, totally." I get tongue-tied, because the guy is seriously intense. "Right here." Crouching, I hit a panel with the side of my fist, causing the hidden door to pop open. Standing, I gesture into the compartment. "Help yourself." His short stature makes it easier for him to make a selection than it does for me to do a squat while pulling bottles out.

The man selects the Lagavulin, placing it on the bar. I can tell by his demeanor that he's from an entirely different culture than the one I was born into. Fetching a clean glass, I serve him, because I doubt the man ever serves himself.

"How many fingers?" I ask, being uber polite.

Toby steps forward, face glowing like a happy puppy, as if he can't help himself. "May I?" Watching in awe as the boy pours the scotch, I realize he takes immense pride in his work, even the smallest of tasks. "Here you go, sir," he murmurs reverently, blushing.

"When did you get in?" I direct to the youngest Klines and their companion, because the older generations are arguing loud enough to eclipse the pounding music. No wonder the man wants a drink or a smoke to deal with their bullshit.

"This afternoon," the man responds for all of them, taking charge. "Dexter Hayes." A hand juts out, and I instinctively place my hand in his.

"Rory Essex," I murmur, voice breaking. "Welcome to my humble club."

"It's nice," Dexter hums, looking around. A ringlet is in the middle of his forehead, and it makes me think of Devon. No way would Dev's OCD allow him to look at Dexter without telling him to push it back into place. "I'm a member of a club in Dominion, New York. Restraint."

"Oh," falls out of my mouth like I'm a dumbass. "I've heard of it." *Holy shit!* Eyes flicking in Toby's direction, more tumblers click into place. "Have you toured the Spook House yet?"

"No, we arrived, had a quick meal, then came directly here," Dexter speaks conversationally, but his unique eyes miss nothing. "It's been a trying day, no doubt turning into a trying night as well."

"Have you spoken to Robin Prynne in private yet?" I lead Dexter in a direction that would make his night epic instead of frustrating.

Cocking his head like a hawk sighting prey, Dexter looks at me yet doesn't reply.

"I suggest you do that," I mutter cryptically, getting tongue-tied by this man's intensity. Just being focused on by this guy makes my heart patter in a panic. "The entertainment you're used to is in the attic of the Spook House. Robin's of your nature, and he's also the keeper of the *inducer of calming effects.*"

Arching a wicked brow in thanks, Dexter salutes me with his glass, then takes a small sip. "May have to lock myself in there while they fight about shit they can never change." He reaches out to rub Toby's back in a possessive touch no one would ever mistake for a platonic gesture.

Dexter Hayes *owns* Tobias Kline.

"Good luck." I kiss Tina on the forehead, then squeeze Toby's bicep, not brave enough to touch him otherwise with his master eyeing me. "If you guys need anything, let me know. My wife's riding shotgun on this train wreck, so if blood and tears are shed, make sure one of them gives us a call."

"It's just going to be hours upon hours of Auggie throwing a tantrum." Tina huffs in disgust. "Big, redheaded child."

"I know Auggie almost as good as you do." I laugh without humor as I grab a handful of water bottles to pass out. "Good luck, girl."

It's another half hour journey to get back to my wife, where I drain two of the bottles of water on my way. "Here– drink up." Plucking a bottle out of my back pocket, I toss it to Ren, and share my opened bottle with Beth. "Having fun?" I purr into Bethany's ear, placing a few soft kisses along her neck.

"Loads," she gasps breathlessly, then goes back to draining her water. "Hot as hell in here, but I'm having a blast."

Hands curving around Beth's hips, I sway her in rhythm to the music thumping in the background. Getting into it with me, she presses her ass against my crotch, tearing a grunt from me. "Gotta hit the head. Too many bottles of water on my way back to ya. Wish me luck getting through the crowd before I piss my pants."

"They love you," she teases, pushing on my belly.

"Not cool, lil pup." Beth's laughter trails behind me as I sneak past our party guests. The bathroom is blessedly empty and a good thirty degrees cooler than the dance floor. Head hitched back, I don't know if I'm moaning because the pressure in my bladder is being alleviated, or because I no longer feel like I'm going to pass out from heatstroke.

"That good, eh?" Devon lurking behind my right shoulder has me shrieking like a little bitch, piss missing the urinal but thankfully not splattering on me.

"Fancy meeting like this again." A sensation of déjà vu descends. "Don't get me hard until I put it away."

"Easier getting a stiffy to fit back into cotton pants." Devon palms my ass, kneading with his fingertips.

I've never pissed so fast in my life, with my cock put away in record time. "Thanks for the gift," I mutter wryly as Devon continues to molest me through the soft pants I'm wearing.

Tugging me away from the rank urinals, Devon pushes me against the far wall. "Only seemed fitting I buy you a gift in celebration of your nuptials to my best friend... a gift that's meant for me to enjoy."

"Having fun?" Nothing could wash the smirk off my face as Devon jams his hands down my pants.

"Oh..." is a breathless rush of a sound. "No boxers. Jesus, Rory. You're killing me here... and no, I wasn't having fun until now. I had to escape my barricade of babysitters. They act like I'm going to jump the bar and pour liquor down my throat. You know it's bad when Essie was telling them to back the fuck off."

Devon's always testing, and he gets off on it. There's something in his brain that derives real pleasure from edging, and not in the sexual sense. Devon pushes himself to the limits, proving he's in control. I'm terrified of the day he finds out his control isn't as strong as he believes. Instead of telling him how proud I am of him for resisting his demons, as he pokes said demons with a stick, I tell him I'll be there should they get the better of him. No judgments. I'll put Devon's confidence back together again.

"They love you," is all I can say. Devon understands it, even if he doesn't like it.

"Do you love me?" Devon murmurs coyly, doing that eyelash flutter he only employs on me. A palm slips deeper into my pants, fingers wrapping around my cock. "Entertain me."

"I'm down for that," spills out my mouth in a sluggish voice. "What do you have in mind?"

Leaning up, Devon bites my bottom lip, then slides back down my body, making sure I feel all of him against me on the way down. Devon's a seductive little shit– sinfully evil.

Fun Devon has no boundaries, and I can't help but follow him straight to hell. Jerking my dick, I've never seen him this turned on before. "Can I fuck you?"

"Yes," spills from my lips without hesitation. Hips jerking forward, I try to get more friction in Devon's fist.

Hitting me with his dark stare, "Or do you want to fuck me?"

Knees weakening, it's a miracle I'm still standing. "Yes."

"Indecisive, are we?" Devon toys with me, and I love every sickening second of it. Get off on it. "Which is it? Hmm… we haven't fucked yet."

"Both," I blurt out. "If I could do both at the same time, I'd probably die of jizz loss."

Laughing that sinful song, Devon half crawls up my body to reach my lips. My hands immediately seek his ass, slipping beneath the soft fabric of his shorts. Palms rolling, I pull him into me.

"Ahem…" A throat clearing has us breaking apart, guilty as sin. "I'm glad to see it's not a zipper emergency, but I'm starting to think you guys find public restrooms an aphrodisiac."

"Shit!" Rubbing at my scalp, I try to will my body to forget about how hot it is, and I don't mean in temperature. "Malcolm… I have no response."

Devon's so turned on, he looks like he's being boiled alive, and he's not sure what to do about it. A guy's father will always be his ultimate sexual kryptonite. Pupils blown, Devon's wigging out– body ready to come, mind screaming *turn it off!*

"I'm gonna go check on Essie." Devon flashes me an apologetic look, because there's no way in hell he can stand in this confined space with his dad when he's this turned on. Too bad I feel the same way.

"Hope you didn't overhear too much." Blushing, I keep rubbing my palms over my scalp.

"Heard plenty," Malcolm clips out, hiding his real reaction. Amusement is trying its damnedest to curl his lips, but he won't show it.

"They know," I stress, making sure the man I respect doesn't think we're cheating on our wives. Watching Devon struggle has me living life to the fullest too, without a lick of guilt or shame. "Devon and I... I have no name for what we are, but our wives know all about it. I know it sounds cheesy, but we feel closer to them. Love them more, if that's possible."

"No judgments from me. So listen–" Malcolm stops me with a palm to my chest. "Before you go, I wanted to say thank you."

Bugging my eyes, "Thank you?" I gulp out.

I'm suddenly thankful I just took a piss, because I've never had this experience before. I never dated girls outside of hooking up at parties as a teenager. No meeting the dad. I already knew James Oman after growing up across the street, so having him for a father-in-law was natural, not stressful.

Right now, I feel like a teenager who just got caught screwing around on the sofa when Dad came home early from work.

"This has probably been one of the most stressful periods in my life, and that's saying something." Malcolm arches an eyebrow, knowing damned well I know all of his business. "There were things Devon's doctor didn't discuss with Devon, but he did with me."

"Like what, a prognosis?" Gut clenching, this conversation is what had Beth sobbing after Devon broke down in front of us on movie night.

"Yes." Malcolm closes his eyes. "Dr. Delaney said Devon was one of the brightest human beings he'd ever met. He was terrified the world would be a dimmer place without Devon in it."

"You're saying Devon's doctor thought he wouldn't survive?" Gulping, panic claws at my insides. Malcolm reaches out to steady me, trying to reassure me.

"*Back then*," Malcolm stresses. "I didn't tell a soul, wanting Devon to have hope. I wouldn't even think it, because I didn't want to admit it to myself. Dr. Delaney said the odds were zero to none of Devon making it to age forty at the time he left Arizona. There were steps Devon refused to take, and I'm sure you recognize how deliberately reckless my son is."

"Yes," I whisper, but refuse to voice how it's one of Devon's more intriguing qualities.

"Recklessness and deviousness are part of Devon's core personality, even though they mirror a manic episode, which makes tracking his moods next to impossible." Sighing, Malcolm slumps against the wall next to me. "A few weeks after Devon got back home, he went postal in the middle of the Batcave."

"I know." Breathing heavily, but finding no air flooding my lungs, I can't get my nerves to calm. I fear Devon feels like this nonstop. "He told me."

"I was terrified, grieving as if Devon was dying before my very eyes. The beginning of the end– the backslide. I called Delaney and put him on speaker phone so he could hear Devon." Snorting, Malcolm shocks the piss out of me with a smirk. "When I finally put the phone to my ear, Delaney was laughing."

"Laughing?" I blurt out, smiling too. "Only Devon would get that reaction."

"Too true." Malcolm huffs a laugh. "It was pure relief. Delaney said he never thought Devon would attack me, because Devon loves me too much. Devon didn't want to hurt me, so he was internalizing his pain and refusing to put the blame on my shoulders. The fact that Devon let it out, and has continued to do so since, had Delaney changing the prognosis."

Hand on Malcolm's arm, "What'd he say?" I rush to get an answer, hoping this panicky fear will dissipate with good news.

"Devon will live a long life, outside of natural disasters, accidents, and natural causes, because he's so goddamn reckless. Delaney feels that even if Devon fucks up, he'll survive the fallout. Devon has the tools now, uses them, and has a voice he wants people to hear."

Falling back against the wall, I take a deep breath for the first time since Malcolm started talking. This is why Beth was terrified. She instinctively recognized the danger Devon was facing, and the pain it was going to cause all of us should it come to pass. For the past few weeks, Beth's been able to concentrate on Auggie, because she trusts Devon again.

Notoriously touchy-feely, Malcolm cups the nape of my neck, drawing me down to kiss my forehead. "Thank you for saving my son," he whispers against my skin, then disappears as quickly as he arrived, locking himself into a stall to collect himself before facing the public.

In a daze, I step out into the hallway, then back up a step when I find my three favorite people waiting for me.

"Thought we'd need reinforcements since you were alone in there with my dad." Sheepish, Devon won't look me in the eye.

Moving quickly, I grab Beth's hand in mine, tugging her along for the ride. Leaning in, I kiss Essie's cheek, then I reach for the bastard who had me feeling like I was dying in the bathroom.

Cupping Devon's face with Beth's fingers still intertwined with mine, I lean in and kiss him, revealing every emotion I feel.

The four of us are woven together.

To lose Devon would weaken us all. We may survive it, but we would never feel alive again. Devon doesn't need stimulants, he doesn't need drugs, because he emits an intoxicating energy that we cannot live without.

"Whoa…" Devon's thick lashes do that fluttery thing. "What was that for?"

"Because I felt like it." Pulling away, I tighten my grip on Bethany's hand– we're in this together. "Everybody doing okay?"

"I'm good." More than halfway drunk, Bethany leans against my shoulder, smiling. "A classmate of mine is doing a case study on relationships featuring two givers, because he believes one will always turn into a taker. No meeting in the middle."

"Yeah?" is more of a question, than a prompt. I notice Essie doesn't seem confused, able to speak Bethany's language.

"Yeah, but I think the four of us are disproving his theory." Pulling my arm over her shoulder, Beth cuddles into my side. "I think as long as we continue to voice what we need, and give it to each other, we're *all* going to be okay," she stresses, pinning Devon with her stare, because he has a propensity to bottle shit up. "My best friends are more important to me than anyone else on this planet. I'll do *anything* to make sure I don't lose a single one of you."

"Oh!" Essie palms Beth's forehead, shoving her. "You always get sappy when you're drunk." It's all an act, because the girl is teary-eyed. Rolling her eyes, "I love you, bitch."

"Right back atcha, slut." Bethany giggles, heavy emotions making her uncomfortable.

Devon and I share a look, not getting how girls call each other derogatory names as an endearment. If I called Devon an asshole, or bastard, or psycho, he'd probably kill me. If he called me one, I'd think he was in a bad mood and I'd leave him be. If either one of us called the girls the names they say to each other, divorce papers would be filed immediately. But the girls are hugging and laughing about things Devon and I will never understand. Which is why Beth tricked me into a blind-friendship-date with Devon in the first place, knowing we both needed this bromance to survive their friendship.

"We should probably get back to the party." Arms hooked, the girls take off down the hallway, chattering up a storm, as if the celebration they organized was just for them.

"Hmm… I feel abandoned for some reason," I mutter wryly, taking up a position next to Devon. Out of respect, we ignore Malcolm as he sneaks out of the bathroom, because the man is the epitome of overemotional– it's that same quality that has our *hugs* rocking Devon's and my worlds. "I could probably bribe Jim at the speedway to let us race our cars after closing. You in?"

"My plan's more fun." A devious light shines up at me, with a sinful smirk curling his lips.

"Enlighten me," I challenge, bumping Devon with my elbow.

"I didn't have a honeymoon–"

"You didn't want one, if memory serves right." The girls so badly wanted to plan a huge wedding, not that Essie wanted a huge one. But Devon was freaking out, so they got married in their backyard by Mayor Ross, with only family and the closest of friends allowed to witness it. Devon's more introverted than he used to be, but I get it. Not a social butterfly, he doesn't need a billion friends. Devon only needs ones who get him.

"You went to Vegas for yours, but it couldn't have been any fun." Devon cuts his dark gaze in my direction, the jealous shit. "I mean, Beth had no one to shop with, and you had no one to gamble with. I'm sure the sex was fantastic, but you needed more fun than that."

"Oh, yeah?" Biting my lip to stifle the laughter threatening to erupt, I watch as the real Devon is revealed. Right now, he's blushing, acting sheepish, and the coyness isn't an act.

"So I bought you a gift–"

"Like my pants?" I banter with him.

"Exactly like the pants," Devon volleys back, smirking smugly. "The gift was to you, but more for me."

"So what gift did you get yourself this time?" Turning to the side, it's taking everything in me not to slam Devon into the wall and suck his face off.

"Four tickets to Vegas," Devon rambles off quickly, confidence dimming. "Leaving tonight."

"Holy shit!" Gasping in wonder, all I can do is stare at the guy who changed my life for the better. "For real?"

"Vegas is filled with stimulation that requires no stimulants." Devon does that eyelash flutter again– this time it's not a seduction technique. "I want to have fun. Live."

"Devon?" I grab his hand because he's starting to fidget, which is never a good sign. His nervousness is palpable, most likely scared I'll reject his gift.

"Yeah?" It's not often Devon shows his vulnerability. The fact that he's revealing it to me, nearly has me suffocating on emotions I never thought I'd feel. It's not the same as I feel for Bethany, but it makes it no less real or important.

If Devon's and my friendship is sinful, then I'll gladly sell my soul to the devil, knowing this path less traveled will be one helluva wild ride.

Drawing our hands to rest against my chest, I make a promise I intend to keep, for all our sakes– for everyone inside Rush's packed club and beyond. We deserve to live in a brighter world because Devon's still in it.

"You trust me, right?" Devon's quick nod is answer enough. "I vow that you will have something to look forward to– *every single day* –for the next seventy years."

Thank you for reading **WOVEN**. Don't miss out on what's to come…

GOOD GIRL, Willow's coming-of-age tale.
WILDLY WEDDED WIFE, Rory & Bethany's novella.
WIDOW, Malcolm & Clover's journey.
WANTON, Opal & Ginny's tasty treat.
WARPED, Devon, Essie, Kieren, & Willow's future.
WOVEN, Rory Essex.
WAGER, Devon takes Rory and the girls to Vegas in Woven's short novella follow-up.
WICKED, Patrick & Lisa Kline (Auggie and Tina's parents)
WAYWARD, Auggie, Isis, and Robin's angsty emotional roller coaster ride.
…and many more to come.

ACKNOWLEDGEMENTS

A lot of work goes into writing a novel, and it isn't just by the writer herself. **My parents:** for their unconditional support. **My readers**: thank you for reading my twisted words and spreading my books to the masses. For without you, no one would've ever heard of my stories. My readers are my lifeblood. A shout out to the members of the **M&M of Restraint Group on Facebook**: thanks for the endless entertainment and inspiration. **Wicked Reads**: (in all its incarnations) **Angela G.**, thank you for taking over and making Wicked Reads better than I could have done by myself. & thank you for helping promote my work and the work of other authors. Angela? Have I told you lately how much I appreciate you? A huge thank you to the **Wicked Writer's Betas** for keeping me grounded and encouraging me to keep trudging along when I get frustrated. Your thoughts and observations are invaluable. ((Hugs)) Beta readers who helped with Woven: **Kris | Angela | Diane | Jacki | Linsey | Alexis | Billie Jo | Tassie | Judith | Jodi Lynn | Jodi |** Someday, I'd love to meet you all in real life– it would be the experience of a lifetime.

ABOUT THE AUTHOR

Erica Chilson does not write in the 3rd person, wanting her readers to *be* her characters. Therefore, writing a bio about herself, is uncomfortable in the extreme.

Born, raised, and here to stay, the Wicked Writer is a stump-jumper, a ridge-runner. Hailing from North Central Pennsylvania, directly on the New York State border; she loves the changes in seasons, the humid air, all the mountainous forest, and the gloomy atmosphere.

Introverted, but not socially awkward, Erica prides herself on thinking first and filtering her speech. There are days she doesn't speak at all. If it wasn't for the fact that she lives with her parents, giving her a sense of reality, she would be a hermit, where the delivery man finds her months after expiration.

Reading was an escape, a way to leave a not-so pleasant reality behind. Reading lent Erica the courage she gathered from the characters between the pages to long for a different life. Writing was an instrument of change, evolving Erica into the woman she is today– a better, more mature, more at peace thinker.

Erica has a wicked mind, one she pours out into her creations. Her filter doesn't allow all of it to erupt, much to her relief. Sarcastic, with a very dark, perverse sense of humor, Erica puts a bit of herself into every character she writes.

I love hearing from readers. If you would like more information on release dates, works in progress, teaser chapters, and random bits of madness, please visit my Facebook Fan Page: https://www.facebook.com/thewickedwriter my website: ericachilson.com or please contact me via email: wickedwriter.ericachilson@gmail.com
DEVIANTS ONLY, if you'd like to join Erica Chilson's closed Facebook group, M&M of Restraint: https://www.facebook.com/groups/MistressandMaster/

www.ingramcontent.com/pod-product-compliance
Lightning Source LLC
Chambersburg PA
CBHW071939170626
46813CB00005B/1792